A Taste of His Own Medicine

A Taste of His Own Medicine

Andrew Hamilton

CROSSWAY BOOKS • WHEATON, ILLINOIS
A DIVISION OF GOOD NEWS PUBLISHERS

A Taste of His Own Medicine.

Copyright © 1993 by Andrew Hamilton.

Published by Crossway Books
         a division of Good News Publishers
         1300 Crescent Street
         Wheaton, Illinois 60187.

Cover illustration: David Yorke

Art Direction / Design: Mark Schramm

First printing 1993

Printed in the United States of America

Library of Congress Cataloging-in-Publication Data
Hamilton, Andrew, 1916-
    A taste of his own medicine / Andrew Hamilton.
        p.   cm.
       1. Family vacations—England—Fiction. 2. Physician—England—
Fiction. I. Title.
PR6058.A55216T37 1993 823'.914—dc20   93-1958
ISBN 0-89107-755-3

01	00	99	98	97	96	95	94	93
15	14	13	12	11	10	9	8	7	6	5	4	3	2	1

Contents

A Letter from Bert   7

Beginnings at Bradham Harbor   21

Viewing the House   29

Love Your Neighbors   42

The Cox'un   56

All the Birds of the Air   60

All the Fun of the Fair   68

A Tall Ship   78

S.O.S.   86

No Fire Without Smoke   97

The Lighthouse   110

The Raising of the *Mary Jane*   128

On the Receiving End   143

Last Appointment   154

A Letter from Bert

It takes something fairly momentous to separate a Scot from his porridge once he's fairly started. But what I'd just read in the letter lying beside my plate brought me up so short that I just sat with spoon suspended in midair. I passed the letter to Elisabeth with a challenging flourish.

"Read that, darling. It's from Bert Pettigrew."

She looked at me inquiringly. Elisabeth is English and regards porridge more as penance than pleasure, and she was now well into her bacon and egg. However, she reluctantly put down her knife and fork, picked up the letter, and read out, "Those dainty-points you gave us are now spreading all over the garden. . . ." She looked up with a mystified frown.

"No, not that bit. Farther down."

She read on, "I thought I'd just let you know that

that little house farther along the Ridge is up for sale. I think it could go fairly cheaply as the old lady who owned it passed away in hospital. She died intestate apparently, and the agents want it off their hands as quickly as possible. There aren't any relatives. The asking price is £16,500, but you should get a thousand off as it needs a good deal of repair. Of course, I don't know if you're still interested."

We had mentioned idly once or twice how nice it would be to have a berth at Bradham Harbor, but it had been very much a pipe dream. There hadn't been any houses available anyway.

Elisabeth looked up at me with a sort of pitying wonder in her eyes as if to say, "Poor old Andy. He must be going round the bend at last. If it were spring, it would be another of his "spring rises!" ("Spring rise" was a family saying for any loony scheme brought on by the bursting out of new life at that season.)

What she said was, "Darling, what are you going on about? We haven't that sort of money."

I smiled one of those smug, superior-knowledge sort of smiles and pushed over my first letter of the morning. It was from the Star Insurance Company informing me of the endowment policy my parents had taken out for me in my infancy and whose small, fixed premium I had taken over when they died. I had almost forgotten about it. That endowment had, with profits, grown to the respectable total of £16,455, for which princely sum I would shortly receive their check. They hoped that I might be inclined to reinvest with them to achieve a yet more grandiose total when

I reached the age of sixty-five. I feared their hopes were going to be disappointed. For a moment, only for a moment, I detected the ghost of a smile flit over Elisabeth's face. It gave me courage, and I went on, but with a studied casualness. "I don't suppose it would do any harm just to pop over and have a look at the place; no need to get involved, of course."

To my astonishment and pleasure she didn't dismiss the suggestion out of hand, but just said nothing. Although I had the peculiar sensation of listening to the replay of an old record, I went on, "I mean, we have got this money which we'd not expected."

It was like the time we were launching into our first house at Wilverton. Only then we hadn't a penny. Unlike me, Elisabeth is a very cautious person. Being the tenth child of an impecunious country parson had bred it into her bones. Our second house, which we'd had built in the large garden of the first with the proceeds of its sale, had given her a lot of heart-searching, but even she had to admit we'd found it an unqualified success—well, almost unqualified. There had been a few hiccups, like blocked land drains and getting flooded out at the back.

We always prayed over decisions, and we both had to feel it was right before we took a big step. It sounds as if we expected God to pick up the tab if things turned out badly, but it wasn't like that. We felt we could trust Him to close a door at the outset if the scheme wasn't in His plan. It prevented vain regrets if the going got tough. But this was very much a one-off situation; it had to be. After all, we didn't *need* two houses, especially when lots of folk hadn't even one, but few of them would find any use for a tiny wooden building miles from a town with no employment near. Yet it was just our cup of tea.

We'd been going to Bradham Harbor to the cottages for years, taking a rented place for a week or so. Cheap though it was compared with flying off to the Costa Brava, it was still quite an annual outlay. If we owned one, not only would it be a sound investment to leave our children in the future, but we could go down rent-free at any time, without having to suit our holiday to a vacant time.

Elisabeth was still holding her fire, so I went on. "You know this is my afternoon off. What do you say we ring up old Bert and see if we could go over and have a look?"

I was again surprised and pleased when Elisabeth said mildly, "Why not? We could take a picnic; it would make a break, and as you say, no harm in taking a look."

I nearly blew it in my excitement. The bit was now between my teeth. "Look," I said, "I'm sure I know that place Bert means. It's that old army hut that's been poshed up to look like a house, and if that poor old lady's been living there for I don't know how long, it's going to take some licking into shape. I bet we could get it for a lot less than they're asking. Just think, the family could go there free, even though we were working, and some of our old mission friends could have a buckshee holiday there. I bet we could let it out too and make it pay the rates and repairs and maybe leave a bit over."

"Steady on!" said Elisabeth. "We're going to have

a look, remember; that's all. Anyway it's time you went to surgery."

I opened my mouth to reply, thought better of it, and meekly went into the hall to get my bag. "I'll ring up Bert from the surgery then," I called back as I opened the front door and shut it quickly behind me.

As I drove the mile to the surgery, I thought about the whole thing. Elisabeth's caution didn't frustrate me. I was so used to her canny approach, and it had saved me from jumping in too soon on numerous occasions. What got on my wick was her inability to spend money on herself. I ought to have been grateful for not having a spendthrift wife, but you can carry economy too far. Her clothes for the most part were so old that the fashion they were made in had come round again. At that very moment she was wearing a pair of our daughter Sarah's cast-off shoes. Sarah was now half a head taller than Elisabeth and had feet to match. I switched to the immediate prospect—the cottage . . . but sight of the surgery gateway brought me to earth with a bump. In the office I greeted Mrs. Banbury, our practice manager.

"Morning, Mrs. Banbury."

"Good morning, Doctor. Full surgery, I'm afraid."

"What's new?"

"Several of your old faithfuls too, Doctor." I made a face, glanced over the post she had put on my shelf, and went into my room. Bradham Harbor, "desirable residences" for sale, and sudden windfalls receded deep into the recesses of my mind. As Mrs. Banbury had intimated, there was a formidable pile of patients' record cards on my table. I guessed about twenty-five.

Here was an assemblage of individual lives in minia-
ture, viewed through a doctor's peephole. Sicknesses,
sorrows, recoveries, homes, children, marital problems—there they were, laid out to the seeing eye and
the interpretative skill of doctors' hieroglyphics, as
confidential as was possible in the practice system.
And a doctor with this minimum aid was expected
to make instant recall of the entire scenario at the
entrance of each patient.

What else were they looking for as they waited
impatiently, resignedly, or grumblingly on the uncomfortable waiting-room chairs for the indicator to flash
and their names to be called? Certainly interested,
undivided attention and, from the Olympian height of
the doctor's knowledge, understanding and percep-
tion, a cure, a solution to their problems, and that at
once—if not sooner, but at least, sympathy. That was
how it seemed to me. Of course there were those who
came with their own diagnosis and treatment already
gleaned from a women's magazine or the telly and
only came to tell me what I was going to do. Also there
were not a few who just wanted a certificate to be off
work for some complaint, real or imagined.

I jerked myself back to the perusal of the first card,
conscious of my cynicism. Like this patient, they all
needed help and were grateful if they got it. I was only
too aware that I was just another fallible human being,
searching for answers and no guru, but with the limited
advantage of training and thirty years of experience.
True, I tried to update my knowledge by attending
post-graduate lectures; I read the reports showered on
us daily—mostly a week late—through the letter-box;

I even managed to sift a little grain from the chaff offered us day by day by pharmaceutical firm reps with their persuaders of ball-point pens, initialled telephone pads, free samples, and invitations to free medical symposia, plus buffet meal, on some malady which, surprise, surprise, responded miraculously and solely to their recently discovered, epoch-making remedy.

Outside behind their counter in the waiting room, our two tame dragons stood on guard. These receptionists were really most undragonlike; they were mature women who had developed through long practice an understanding and sympathetic relationship with the patients, but they could be tough when the occasion demanded it. The attempts by would-be queue-jumpers to get a nonurgent consultation without appointment were courteously blocked. They knew that we could only give each patient an average of five or six minutes if we were to get through in time to do our visits, and they were quite capable of dealing with trouble-makers, but still able to pick out frightened and needy folk as well. They earned their salaries.

I pressed the button on my desk. It made a buzz in the waiting room and lit up my name on the indicator. There was a pause, then a knock on my door.

"Come in. Ah, good morning, Mrs. Elwood. Sit down; now what is the trouble?"

"Well, doctor, I don't know whether I ought to be worrying you. It's such a little thing, but I've noticed recently that my bowels haven't been working regularly, and then this morning I saw some blood. I don't suppose it's anything to bother about, but I would appreciate it if you could tell me that everything is all right." A tiny alarm bell started ringing in my head, but I wanted to get a full history of her condition before jumping to conclusions. After a number of questions, I rang for Mrs. Banbury. She took Mrs. Elwood into the examination room, got her undressed, and then called me in. The checkup confirmed my initial suspicion. She had a growth in the back passage. I calmly informed her, "Mrs. Elwood, you have a small obstruction. We will need to do further tests. Would you be agreeable for a letter to go into hospital for an X-ray and to be seen by a consultant? After that we will know what needs to be done."

She had always been a woman of great composure and now, without a quaver in her voice, she asked, "Doctor, have I got cancer? I would like you to tell me straight out."

"I truly cannot answer that. You have a lump; whether it is malignant or not can't be said until after the X-ray and the specialist's examination and opinion. I promise you that I won't deceive you. Whatever the trouble is, I will tell you."

She dropped her eyes, and the corners of her mouth quivered. Then compressing her lips, she stood up. "Thank you, Doctor." She walked with a firm step to the door. Sometimes it is almost intolerable having to wreck someone's peace of mind. If only I could have said to Mrs. Elwood what had been said to me under not very different circumstances, "Nothing to worry about. Eat plenty of fiber. Good-bye." I silently said a prayer for this fine lady, heaved a sigh, and pressed the buzzer again.

Two hours later I was picking up the last card, and by now I was feeling like a sucked orange. Constantly readjusting the old brain to each new case was draining. I pressed the buzzer for the last time. The name on the card was Doubleday.

Double time it ought to be, I thought ruefully. Usually I didn't mind this chap, but this had been quite a morning—almost . . . normal in fact!

Mr. Doubleday was a genial soul and a remarkably healthy one, an early-retired widower who had only just given up playing hockey when they couldn't find him a place even on the Wilverton third team. Time hung a little heavy on his hands, and I guessed he only came to the surgery for the social contact. He always reminded me of the story of the waiting-room patient who said to his neighbor, "Haven't seen you here recently." The other replied, "No, I 'aven't been well enough."

Mr. Doubleday must be running short of symptoms. He was reduced to complaining of backache at bowls (which had now replaced hockey). He usually booked in for the end of the surgery on the supposition that "the last shall be (as the) first," only a bit more so as the heat was off. Today he had managed to get a thorn in the thumb, achieved while pruning the roses. By the time I had got it out, I was simply gasping for that cup of coffee.

"Thanks, Doc," he said and undid a small parcel that he had left on a chair by the examination couch. "Thought your missus might like this." It was a beautiful little red cyclamen in a pot. He walked out before I had time to thank him and left me feeling quite a heel.

I tottered out into the safety of Mrs. Banbury's office and collapsed on her spare chair. She glanced up at me from her typing. "Get you a coffee, Doctor?"

"Thanks."

While she was out in our little kitchen, I sat and considered how much the practice owed to her ministrations. Apart from arranging staff duties, she looked after accounts, typed letters, ordered drugs, masterminded surgery functions, interviewed would-be patients anxious to join the seven thousand we already had, tested specimens in our mini-laboratory, and chaperoned female patients requiring examinations, *and* she had never been known to grumble. A paragon indeed! She brought in my coffee with a couple of biscuits and returned quietly to her typing. As I sipped it slowly, for it was pretty hot, I suddenly remembered I was going to phone Bert Pettigrew. "Could I borrow your phone, Mrs. Banbury?" She pushed the set over towards me.

I dialed Bert's Bradham Harbor number. There was no reply for a minute or two. Then I heard Bert's voice, "Bert Pettigrew here." He sounded breathless.

"Hello, Bert; this is Andrew."

"Oh, sorry not to answer more quickly. I was down in the garden." Where else? If he hadn't been there, I would have been concerned for his health, for he and his wife Jean pretty well lived "down in the garden."

"Ringing up about that house, were you, Doc?"

16

he went quickly on. "Well, it's still got its board out-side; are *you* interested?"

"Yes, we are," I said with studied calm. "Could you tell me a bit more? Who are the agents, and do you think an offer of fifteen thousand would be consid-ered? It's not really derelict, is it? I mean, if we worked on it ourselves, we could get it habitable, couldn't we?"

At the other end Bert laughed. "One thing at a time, Doc. Now the agents are Mooring and Fishway— they're in Bradham. I've got their number; hang on, here it is—Bradham 4156. They have an office on High Street. I should give 'em a ring and see when you can see the place—that is, if you really want to go ahead. And, yes, I do think it's worth offering fifteen thou-sand. They always ask over the odds, as you know, and, honestly, the poor old girl had let the place run down a bit. But you wouldn't think so from the ad in the *Bradham Advertiser*; it says, "Charming timber-frame bungalow in much sought-after situation. Somewhat in need of redecoration; parking space for car and boat, if desired; extensive garden." I suppose you could get a car in, if it were a mini, and I suppose you could get a dinghy in too somewhere. They don't mention that the sea is a quarter of a mile away, and you'd have to carry the boat! *And* they don't tell you that the extensive garden is mostly composed of shin-gle! The only way they dare ask a figure like this is sim-ply because this *is* a unique area. It can't be built on, and there's nothing between it and the sea except a field and the sea wall, as you know—what with its being an S.S.S.I. (Site of Special Scientific Interest) and protected. Some people will pay the earth for all that. I'm sure you could get the house shipshape and Bristol fashion yourselves, but it'd take time; can you spare it?"

"Could be. Well, I'll give Mooring and Fishway a ring, Bert. If they can arrange it, Elisabeth and I could come over this afternoon. I've got it off, so we'd see for ourselves."

"Good, and come and have a cup of tea with us afterwards."

"Thanks, we'll do that. Bye, Bert."

I put the phone down and looked under my eyebrows across the table at Mrs. Banbury. She was looking at her notes and had been typing again, but there was a faint quizzical smile playing around her lips. I could guess what she was thinking.

Here we go—another wild scheme! Mrs. Banbury was a good ally of Elisabeth's in the job of keeping me in order.

"Just making some general inquiries about a holiday bungalow, Mrs. Banbury," I threw at her nonchalantly.

"Oh, yes, Doctor?" There was a wealth of meaning in those three words. Translated they meant, "I've heard that one before; for goodness sake, play it cool and look before you leap. Think about the long-term involvement."

I put through the call to Mooring and Fishway. Yes, they would be able to see us at half past two. I read through the letters Mrs. Banbury had typed, signed them, and got up. She looked at me apologetically.

"I'm sorry, Doctor, there's just one visit for you."

"But, Mrs. Banbury, you know it's my afternoon off."

"I know, Doctor, but it's for Mrs. Fairbairn, and she asked especially for you. Said you would know all about her."

"Yes, I do know Mrs. Fairbairn." It would have been strange if I hadn't, considering the pullover I was wearing. It was so bright people shaded their eyes when the sun was on it. She had first come to see me with a strange tiredness after flu. I found she had a patch of pneumonia at the base of the right lung.

We got her better with antibiotics and physiotherapy, and when she came back, she said she'd like to knit me a pullover. She didn't say why, but I noticed she looked rather fixedly at the one I was wearing; I mean, after five years the best pullovers begin to look a bit tatty.

Today I found her looking very ill.

"It's this pain in my right side, Doctor," she said.

I tapped round her chest and listened with my stethoscope. No doubt about it, she now had fluid around the right lung. Apleural effusion. "Mrs. Fairbairn, that right lung's making trouble again. You've got some fluid there, and I'm afraid you may have to pop into hospital to have it drained off." I spoke as cheerily as I could, though in my heart I was wondering whether there was anything more sinister behind this setback.

"Oh, Doctor, I'm afraid! I have a horror of the hospital. My husband died there."

"I understand, Mrs. Fairbairn." I held her hand as I would a child's. "You know, it's not a proper operation. It's just putting a needle into your chest under a local anesthetic; you'll hardly feel it." But the fear remained in her eyes, and her grip on my hand was like a vice.

"Do you trust yourself to our care, Mrs. Fairbairn?"

"Oh, Doctor, I do, but . . ."

"Can you trust yourself in God's hands? He cares even more for you than we do." She lifted her eyes; she was more composed now, but there was still that hunted look.

"I'll try, Doctor."

"Have you ever seen a baby *trying* to trust its mother's arms? What does it have to do? Try? No, it just rests. Do you know the verse in the Bible that says, 'underneath are the everlasting arms'? Don't *try* to trust—just rest."

I saw her into the ambulance and then went back to my car.

Beginnings at Bradham Harbor

Elisabeth had the picnic lunch all ready when I got home. As she put it all in the basket, she said, "Are you all set to go now, Andy? No visits?"

"I had one—had to send a nice old lady into the hospital, but that's all."

I could see that she was really looking forward to an afternoon out. Most days she had to stick around the home a good deal of the time to pick up emergency calls.

We took the road inland; Elisabeth loved our Sussex countryside. We soon left Wilverton behind and climbed steadily on to the Downs, mellow in the autumn sunshine and dotted with sheep. There had been some days of rain, and the grass had recovered some of its spring greenness. We just tooled along gently, for there was no hurry, and I knew the road like the back of my hand. By the time we passed by Brighton, we were more than halfway to Bradham. Then using the by-roads, we skirted Eastbourne on high ground still. Soon we dropped down towards the great stretch of reclaimed marshland, intersected below us by water-filled drainage ditches, and there was Bradham a few miles ahead, sitting on its own little hill.

It was a good place to have lunch. As soon as we saw an opening, we pulled off the road. There was a grassy patch under the lee of a stout hawthorn hedge. We parked the car on it and spread a ground sheet and a tartan blanket near the hedge. The narrow country lane ran downhill, and from our picnic site we could look southwards to the deep blue of the English Channel.

While Elisabeth got the food out, I opened the boot and extracted our camping secret weapon—our amazing "volcano" kettle. Two years before I had been beguiled by an advert in a camping magazine which appealed to my Scottish instincts. According to the claims, you could boil nearly two pints of water using only a newspaper for fuel! I didn't really believe it, but it only cost, I think, thirty shillings. So I got one from a camping shop and—it worked! The kettle consisted of two cones of aluminum about fourteen inches high, one inside the other, sealed top and bottom, leaving the space for the water between. There was a chimney up the middle, open top and bottom, and a plugged filling and pouring spout at the top. There was a stand for the kettle with a gap where you could push in fuel, rolled-up newspaper or even dry grass and leaves. When the fuel was lit, the flames and smoke went up the chimney, pouring out at the top, giving a very good imitation of a mini-volcano. Literally, with one *Daily Telegraph*, one match and the water, I could make a full pot of tea in five minutes, faster than the liquid gas stove.

On this occasion, Elisabeth's enthusiasm was somewhat muted. Unfortunately, I had commenced my tea-making exhibition to windward, and the little breeze caused her to become suddenly enveloped in a cloud of smoke from the burning *Telegraph*. With considerable dexterity I removed the flaming apparatus to a second eruption site to leeward. With the paper entirely consumed, it remained only for me to scatter the ash widespread, and all traces of our fiery tea-making were removed, except for a circle of scorched turf where the volcano had been. Sometimes I wondered whether local inhabitants suspected strange occult rites when they found curious blackened rings scattered about the countryside in our wake.

After lunch we lay back, comfortably replete, under the lee of the hedge, contemplating the sky and remembering how we had discovered Bradham Harbor on a day just such as this years before. A host of half-forgotten happenings came back.

"We weren't looking for anything in particular," remembered Elisabeth. "It was your afternoon off, and just like now we were simply pottering around. Pete was at boarding school, and Sarah and Barney weren't due out 'til four o'clock. It was you who saw the signpost for Bradham, so we went through slowly without stopping. Then we saw a sign "To Bradham Harbor," and you would go there too, always wanting to see somewhere else, never satisfied."

"Yes, but it turned out worthwhile, didn't it? You have to admit it."

It had certainly started something. When we got to the harbor, that was the end of the road, so we turned down a side road on to the quayside. We had a picnic sitting on some crates and watching crew members unloading a small cross-channel boat with boxes of French produce. There were about half a dozen fishing boats too, all moored up like the cargo boat on the mud of the Bradey River mouth because the tide was out.

After lunch we'd wandered back down the street past the church—a Victorian Gothic building but not out of keeping, surprisingly unornate and built of Kentish rag, the village store which appeared to be selling everything from floor polish to ice cream, and an even smaller shop advertising locally made pottery. Across the main street we saw a sign pointing down a stony track which said, "The Ridge-Private Road. Locked gate ahead. Footpath to nature reserve."

"Let's have a look," said Elisabeth. As we walked slowly down the track, we saw on the left a broad field grazed by a small flock of Romney Marsh sheep. Beyond that lay the shingle sea wall and beyond that, the sea. To the right was a row of widely spaced bungalows, mostly built of wood, but some had brick additions. They looked from their ramshackle appearance to be survivors from early days when all sorts of shanties could be built as holiday homes without the rigid control that came later. They stood on a shingle ridge about six feet higher than the road. Behind, the "gardens" dropped down rapidly to the level of the surrounding grassland. This ridge must have been originally a further defence against the inroads of the ocean.

We'd gone a hundred yards when the track ended abruptly in a wire fence, a stile, and yet another notice which read, "Nature Reserve. Keep to the footpath. No entry to the main reserve without permit—obtainable from Warden, Main Street, Bradham Harbor." We remembered we'd seen a cottage labeled Warden, and we had wondered, "Warden of what?" The path ran diagonally across the field towards the sea wall. It was bordered by an electric fence with a warning notice, "Electrified—keep dogs away."

We climbed the stile and began to cross the field. There ahead was yet another notice, "Keep dogs strictly on a lead." The field had another flock of sheep feeding in it.

"Fond of notices around here," I said.

"So would you be if you had a public footpath running across a sheep field," said Elisabeth.

At length we were scrambling over the sea wall. The tide was in, and the sea winked and sparkled almost at our feet. We walked slowly along the narrow strip of sand, from time to time stopping to send a flat stone skimming away over the sea but keeping our eyes on the tide edge with memories of "swag" collected in the past, including a large unopened tin of Nescafe. Here there were only lumps of driftwood and endless plastic bottles with French labels.

At last we turned, walked back and sat, leaning

against a breakwater out of the wind for a few moments before dawdling back down the track. We looked closely at the bungalows. The one at the end nearest the stile was a most original structure. Why hadn't we noticed it before? It was made out of two antediluvian railway carriages linked by a wooden porch.

"Look at that! D'you see? The doors are still there for the first-, second-, and third-class carriages. There haven't been three classes since the twenties!" I said. The gold lettering, though dimmed with age and weathered, was legible. "My hat!" I read the notice at the gate, "'Holiday Residence. Summer Lets. Inquiries—Tel. Ranford 23359.' Darling, are you thinking what I'm thinking?"

"I hope not," replied Elisabeth.

"You know, this could be the answer for our Bible class camp."

"Knowing our boys, I'd say the owners would need their heads examined if they contemplated letting it to us," she said coolly.

"Oh, come on! They aren't as bad as that. Anyway, it looks the sort of dump that even the boys would have difficulty spoiling. There's nobody in residence. Let's have a look."

In spite of her caustic and, I'm afraid, only too rational comments, Elisabeth was just as keen as I was to see what it was like. We went cautiously up the short steep drive and, just in case someone was there after all, knocked on the door. When no one came, we wandered round and looked through the carriage windows. As far as we could see through the encrusted sea salt, they were all the same, no matter what the class. In each there were some bunk beds, a table, and two chairs—and that was all. In the back we found a sizable brick extension, not visible from the front. This comprised a large living room, again sparsely furnished, a kitchen, a bathroom, and loo. In the kitchen was a gigantic slow-burning cook stove.

"It would do—just," said Elisabeth, "but it would be pretty cramped. Of course we could put up some tents at the back and bring some chemical loos as well. Ye-es, it would do, but of course if they hear who's going to inhabit it, they won't agree. You can bet on that!"

"No harm in having a bash. We'll tell 'em about the boys, and if they agree—we're away."

Elisabeth still looked doubtful. In spite of her reluctance, I felt encouraged that she was talking like someone already involved in the project and not as a mere critical onlooker. Since our return from a mission to Africa many years before, Elisabeth had had to contend with ill health. While she was a tremendous standby in the home, she did not often feel fit enough to be in the front line of our "extra-mural" activities. But now she was saying, "*We*" could put up some tents. . . ." If she felt able to supervise the domestic side of the exercise, we were virtually home and dry— what with our daughter Sarah and some of her friends helping and our right-hand man, Mickey, a young accountant and his wife to do our timetable and run the games. There was still the matter of getting permission to use the cottage, of course.

As soon as we got back home that night, we phoned. No, the house wasn't booked that Whitsun.

No, they had no objection to the boys provided they were well behaved. They had had parties of boys before (*not like ours though*, I thought, while stifling my conscience and determining to keep the little blighters under strict control, even if it killed me).

Taking it all in all, it had turned out a successful camp in spite of the weather. It must have been the first Whitsun for years that it snowed three inches to start with and then had temperatures in the mid-seventies for the rest of the time. We played cops and robbers, tracking through the snow on the first day, and then reverted to our time-honored game of crocker . . . and that is where Jamie McFee came into his own. Jamie was a boy of thirteen with two left hands and no ball sense but an indomitable will. He was a trier, and he tried the patience of most of his side. He was always late starting to run and consequently ran out half of them. Yes, apart from Jamie, who was always looking out the window during our talks and discussions on the Christian life, camp *was* a success. *And* we couldn't have harmed the house much, for we were welcomed back there year after year. It was during this time that we had the good fortune to get to know Bert Pettigrew and his wife Joan. They helped us a lot in practical ways. It was through him that we first rented another cottage for ourselves during the summer months for a more restful holiday with our own family.

But it was time to end the recollections and be on our way. We stood up, virtuously made sure we hadn't left any litter, and then put the things back in the car and started off again.

Viewing the House

Our first port of call was Bradham, perched on its hilly promontory. It had once been a port, for in the dim and distant past, the sea had lapped its very base. But now the town lay a mile inland. By ten past two I was edging the car along its narrow streets. We found Mooring and Fishway's office easily enough, down opposite the museum on the main street not far from the ancient church. We stopped by the roadside and sat in the car, waiting for the church clock to strike the half-hour.

We loved this place, second only to the harbor itself. It was a fascinating town, much older than the harbor, having begun in the thirteenth century. We often popped in there when we were on holiday at the harbor, especially on wet days, for the museum had a fine collection of historical relics from both war and peace. Sometimes we would wander round the ancient church where the kaleidoscope of colors from the stained glass of the windows fell on the many sarcophagi.

On our very first proper visit we noticed in a side chapel one large marble tomb. The inscription, which I laboriously translated from my rudimentary knowledge of Latin, acquired to qualify for entry into Cambridge University, informed us that here lay the mortal remains of one Sir Edgar Balno and his wife. Their effigies lay coldly side by side upon the marble top. He had been the lord of the manor of Bradham and, indeed, had been the last of his line, having died childless in 1542.

Sadly, in his later life, he seemed to have accumulated several blots on his reputation. These were not of a moral, but of a mental nature; to put it bluntly, he had lost his marbles. The gentleman embarked on a series of expensive and futile ventures.

It really was all the fault of the French. It had been their custom for many years to cross the Channel to attack, pillage, and burn the town. Sir Edgar naturally objected to this, especially when his own mansion was once badly damaged. So under Henry VIII's patronage, he had built a small but strong and well-armed fort to guard the harbor. The heaviest cannons available pointed seawards from the battlements, and only the most avaricious and foolhardy French vessel would have dared approach. Alas, for years the shingle had begun building up at the old mouth of the Bradey, and a series of storms finally blocked passage to all shipping. Soon a mile of salt marsh separated

Bradham from the sea. So the French came no more, and an expensive and redundant castle stood a monument to his mistaken foresight.

Apart from this gaffe, he had financed the building of large and expensive cellars under Bradham's rebuilt houses whence to store imported wine—in the hope that peace might allow the wine trade from the continent to resume. But as there was no port, no wine, and no profits, Sir Edgar himself fell into a decline and died, his memorials a brand-new, unused fort and a lot of empty vaults. A friend of mine had bought one of the houses and had found a use for its redundant vault—as a Ping-Pong room.

The church clock chimed the half hour. When we opened the door to Mooring and Fishway, an old-fashioned bell on a coiled spring triggered off and jangled again as we closed the door. The room we had entered was not without charm despite its atmosphere of musty shade. The dim light from the diamond-paned windows revealed cream-plastered walls and dark oak beams. A tall, cadaverous man with thinning gray hair and wispy side whiskers rose from behind a heavy desk and extended his hand.

"Dr. and Mrs. Hamilton?"

"That's right. How do you do?"

"Fishway, madam and sir, Fishway. I trust you had a comfortable journey here, a comfortable journey?" By the way he said it we might have just traveled from the north of England.

"Yes, thank you. I expect you know we have come about the sale of the bungalow on the Harbor Ridge."

"Of course, of course. Seascape, to be sure. I have

the details here, just here." He handed each of us a typed sheet from a folder on his desk. "But please sit down; do sit down.

"Well now, as you can see, a very fair little property, very fair indeed. But the situation, ah now, the situation! That is unique, quite unique. No other building possible, quiet road, view straight out to sea; not many properties can offer that; likely to excite a lot of interest, sir, a lot of interest."

I felt drawn to this survivor from an age of courtesy. I realized that his habit of repeating himself was not an affectation. It was more to reassure himself and maintain his poise. I felt he was at heart a retiring man.

"Have you had many offers so far?" I asked, innocently enough.

"Well, no, nothing definite, but of course the property has just come on the market. They will come, oh yes, they will come. You may count on that." This was encouraging. We were evidently first in the field. Again I felt a liking for this elderly man. I was ready to do business with him; he might not be slick, but he was honest. Most other house agents would have told us that several other offers were being considered.

"Do you think we could see the property straight away? We have to return to Wilverton this evening."

"Certainly, certainly, I have the keys here." He produced a small bunch from the table drawer.

"Would you be agreeable to seeing the property by yourselves? My partner, Mr. Mooring, you see, is now showing a gentleman around another property, and as we are short of a secretary at the moment, I am left in charge of the shop. Yes, in charge of the shop!"

He gave a genteel chuckle, fingers placed delicately over his mouth and his head on one side. Secretly I was glad. We could now poke around on our own to our heart's content.

"You will find some quite good period furniture in the house. It is included in the price—all included." I noticed he had not specified which period. Late Victorian, I guessed, or at least before World War I.

"The rooms, I am afraid you will find rather disheveled, yes, distinctly disheveled. The previous owner, very elderly, you know, very elderly indeed, and the house had been left empty—the lady in the hospital. Sad, very sad."

"That's all right, Mr. Fishway. We quite understand. I think I remember the old lady. Mrs. Winscale, wasn't it? Rather a dear." He smiled and nodded. "We shall be back in an hour or so to return the keys."

"Thank you, sir, thank you." He shook us both by the hand and opened the door for us. The door jangled its farewell, and the light in the street dazzled our eyes for a moment after the gloom of the office.

"I bet that under that benign, old-world manner beats a true house agent's heart," I said briskly. "But he's got his living to make like the rest of us. We'd better get going."

"Hold on. We ought to take a little something to the Pettigrews, love," said Elisabeth.

"Well, what do you suggest? Not much scope in a village this size."

"Let's try there." She pointed down the street to a village store housed in another oak-beam-and-plaster building. We found a delicatessen offering smoked trout, home-cured ham, German sausage, a huge uncut Gorgonzola cheese, and at least ten different sorts of coffee beans in jars. The beans could be roasted and ground on the premises. A cloud of aromatic blue smoke greeted us outside the door, filtering through a ventilator from the roaster revolving in a corner, blue flame flickering beneath the perforated cylinder.

Even with this exotic array of foodstuffs, it wasn't easy to get something special for the Pettigrews. They were very nearly vegetarians. A meal there was, well, *unusual*, but very enjoyable too, all barring their "tea." It wasn't really tea but some noncaffeine-containing South African weed which, even when masked with honey and lemon, still tasted like the smell of Cherry Blossom boot polish.

"There, that will do." Elisabeth pointed to a punnet of out-of-season strawberries on a stand. There was nothing rural and country about the price. Carrying the bag as if it contained a porcelain vase, Elisabeth led the way back to the car. Next moment we were running down a steep slope out of the village by the castle to the road across the levels, first beside the re-channeled Bradey River and then in a straight line towards the sea. Vast fields stretched away to our right, on and on to the high ground which ended abruptly in hundred-foot cliffs dropping to the shore at the distant point. Low farm buildings lay in the middle of the recovered marshland, sheltered from the prevailing winds by a stand of old pollarded willows. Tucked under the lee of the high ground lay a nature reserve with a bird sanctuary, a lake which had once been a gravel pit, and demonstration buildings which had once been barns.

As we coasted along, a cloud of curlew flew over our heads, landed in the fields, and began probing the ground with their long curved beaks. Their haunting cry, "Coor-lee," never failed to thrill us. It brought back memories of the wild, high, open lands of North Wales as well as the lush marshlands of the south.

At the harbor we turned off along the Ridge track and began picking our way around potholes to pull up at last on the grass verge outside Seascape. We walked up the short path and stood for a moment outside the front door to look over the field to the sea wall and the sea. On the horizon a huge tanker moved almost imperceptibly to the west, standing high out of the water, its tanks emptied at an oil terminal somewhere in the Thames estuary. We unlocked the door, but it was stuck. I had to lift it bodily before I could open it.

"Good start!" I said to Elisabeth. "Sagging hinges. Let's see what the rest of the place is like." When I pulled the curtains to let in some light, I went off into explosive sneezes at the cloud of dust motes dancing away in the sunlight.

We wiped off the furniture with some dusters which we took from the kitchen table drawer and dampened. From the walls, pictures of Highland cattle, a print of Constable's *Haywain*, and several sepia photographs of venerable ancestors looked down at us. The women had on tight black bodices, and the gentlemen were standing with hands thrust into high-lapelled jackets, their mutton-chop-whiskered faces gazing threateningly into the middle distance.

"I don't know who looks the fiercer, the men or

the Highland cattle," said Elisabeth. The furniture was "period" all right—heavy, Victorian, and shabby, but it really was quite eminently serviceable, especially for folk like us who put comfort before poshness. A couple of old armchairs with high backs, curved mahogany arms, and uncut moquette-covered padding were hard but comfortable, and there was a three-seater sofa with an end let down by pressing a knob on the outside.

"We had one like this at home," I said to Elisabeth, dropping it down and putting it back a few times with nostalgic pleasure.

"Stop doing that and come and look at the kitchen," Elisabeth commanded.

I pushed the end back into place and meekly followed her. She should have said "kitchen-dining room," for that was what it was—with a deal table and four deal chairs in the middle, a white earthenware sink and an ancient electric cook stove at one end, and a dresser and door into a larder at the other. Dishes still stood in the rack on the draining board by the sink, and the lino-covered floor was sticky with grease.

"Poor old dear. She must have been taken off in a hurry; this is obviously just as she left it when she went to hospital."

Elisabeth put the dishes in their places on the dresser. I was callously examining the walls for cracks. They weren't too bad. The combined bathroom and loo, contrary to modern regulations, led off from the kitchen. It was a pleasant surprise—it had modern fittings, but there was a high-water mark left round the bath. Another modern concession was the immersion

36

heater. I went through the back door and walked around the house, leaving Elisabeth to examine the two bedrooms. As I went along, I stuck my penknife here and there into the timber cladding of the walls. The extensive rot in the boarding I put down to age and neglect. With the house standing on six feet of pebbles, it could hardly be due to rising damp, but the place had not been painted for years. Still it mightn't be too bad; the boarding could be renewed, provided the timber framing wasn't rotted too. We would have to strip off the cladding and see. But we'd have to be careful; we didn't want the whole place collapsing about our ears. I was forgetting one thing of course— we hadn't bought it yet.

Elisabeth stuck her head out the back door. "Come on, love, 'bout time we took that cup of tea off the Pettigrews." She looked quite fetching with cobwebs draping her hair.

It was real tea Jean served this time, Earl Grey laid on especially for us, with home-made scones and honey in the comb from their hives. As we ate, I noticed Jess the dog looking hopefully at my biscuit, but I knew their rules, hardened my heart, and stuck the last bit into my mouth.

After a little I stood up. "We ought to get back to old Fishway's before they close up. Thank you very much for the tea. We'll offer the fifteen thousand and see what gives. We'll let you know."

Ten minutes later we were standing once again inside the dim office in Bradham High Street.

"Thank you for the keys, Mr. Fishway." I handed them back.

"Well, Doctor, and did you come to any decision, my dear sir?"

"Mmm, we liked the house, but it needs a lot of work. There is quite a bit of rotten timbering, and it needs complete redecoration inside and out. We are prepared to offer £15,000, but that is our limit, and I really *mean* that, Mr. Fishway, so you will have to tell the vendors just that."

I looked him straight in the eye, but he was giving nothing away. All he said, very courteously, was, "Thank you, Doctor. I'm sure you will realize that that is considerably less than the asking price, considerably less. But I will forward your offer and let you know their response as soon as possible."

"Thank you, Mr. Fishway. We'd be grateful. I'm afraid we'll have to push on now. We'll wait to hear then." I put out my hand, and he shook it genially and then shook hands with Elisabeth as well.

"Good-bye. You shall hear from me soon, very soon. Good-bye." He graciously preceded us to the door and opened it for Elisabeth.

I turned and said once more, "Sorry to repeat it, Mr. Fishway, but I really mean that £15,000 is our limit." He bowed and smiled graciously as I followed Elisabeth out. The door shut behind us with the usual jangle of the bell.

We drove about twenty miles in silence. I guessed Elisabeth was already feeling we'd taken the plunge too easily. I was too, but the thought mingled with the worry that we *could* have left the door open for just a *little* increase. . . .

Then my jaw set. NO! It was quite enough for a

jerry-built little house wherever it was situated. If by a long shot our offer were accepted, we'd need most of the spare cash from my endowment insurance to do the repairs and fit the place up well enough to let it to outsiders. Would the offer be accepted? Now that the excitement of negotiating was over, it all felt a bit flat.

"We'll just have to wait and see," I said, as if that were a most profound conclusion. Elisabeth glanced across the car at me. Her voice was kind and gentle. She always reads me like a book.

"Of course, darling, but we can have peace about it. If we're not meant to have Seascape, then they won't accept our offer, and we'll know it just wasn't God's will." Of course, she was right, but the matter-of-fact way she was taking things grated on me. I *wanted* them to accept our offer, and I was going to be very disappointed if they didn't.

I felt better that night when we'd finished a late high tea and had our evening Bible reading and prayer together. I slept well after all that fresh air, but I dreamed of a wonderful mansion by a beautiful coast. Mixed up in the dream were old memories of the past. All the family including the grandchildren were there; we wandered happily along the beach watching gulls picking winkles off the rocks, flying up and dropping them, then swooping down to gobble the winkles from the broken shells. Then an Arctic skua came floating in, harrying the gulls until they disgorged their hard-won food, which the skua caught like a juggler in midair.

I woke myself up in the dawn by saying hoarsely,

"Not a penny more, not a penny more." The mansion and the sea coast were already receding into the haze.

That day the surgery was shorter than usual. I was in Mrs. Banbury's office writing down calls in my visiting book when a call came through from Elisabeth. We had an unwritten rule that she didn't contact me unless there was an emergency or unless someone had phoned there for a visit by mistake. She normally had a lovely alto voice, but it sounded now quite high-pitched and strange.

"Darling, Mr. Fishway has just rung. They've accepted our offer!"

"Yippee!" I couldn't help it. Mrs. Banbury stared at me.

"That's marvellous. Thanks, love, we'll talk about it at dinner time. Bye." Mrs. Banbury was still glancing at me questioningly.

"Good news, Doctor?"

Belatedly I assumed a nonchalant air again. "Could be. You remember I mentioned a holiday bungalow yesterday? Well, my wife liked it and so did I, so we put in a tentative bid well below their asking price and—they've accepted it."

Mrs. Banbury frowned slightly. "A bit funny their taking your offer below the price. Are you sure there isn't some major defect in the building?"

I threw all reticence to the winds. "Mrs. Banbury, we went over it with a fine-tooth comb. Sure, there's lots that's wrong with it, but after all, it's just a wooden building. O.K., it needs work, but you pay for what you get, a *pied à terre*, and if it's stood there since the first world war, it'll stand there for a bit yet."

She smiled. "Will you be able to use it this summer?"

"That's the idea. When we get it set to rights, you **are** going to come out with your husband and see it. It really is in a peach of a spot. From the front you can see across a field and over the sea wall to the Channel, and at the back over the meadows to Bradham on the hill. Our elder son is mad about birdwatching, and there's the bird sanctuary a short walk away. The beach is almost deserted most of the year, and it's lovely sand for the kids."

"Sounds just right," she said kindly.

Love Your Neighbors

The driftwood burned in the old-fashioned cast-iron grate with a bright blue flame and an occasional crackle and spit. Someone, probably Bert, had gathered it in the spring for old Mrs. Winscale, and it was the salt in it that gave the flame its sapphire tinge. Elisabeth was sitting quietly in one of the fireside chairs, and I was nearly asleep in the other. It had been a full day. After a packed surgery, I had driven the forty miles from Wilverton, and now a good supper of boiled eggs, toast, cornflakes, and apples—all washed down with Keemun tea—had produced a pleasant state of euphoria. The dirty dishes were still on the draining board waiting for me. Elisabeth was bent over her writing case, "keeping in touch with the family." Tomorrow we would get down once more to the daunting task of renovating Seascape.

All that winter we had been bashing away at it, usually from Friday evening to Saturday night on my weekends off, returning early on Sunday to Wilverton for church and the afternoon boys' Crusader class. Slowly but surely we were winning, but our program depended on the weather forecast. When it said it would be fine, we reckoned that heavy rain would force us inside and vice versa when the forecast was appalling.

This particular Saturday was cold but sunny, so I had worked outside and Elisabeth within. Things were taking shape, rather an odd shape at times. My carpentry, I was sure, would last, but it was on the crude side. Bit by bit I had stripped the rotted outside boarding and to my great relief found the timber frame underneath still sound. A local timber yard had dumped a load of weather boarding in the front garden, and gradually I was getting the gaps measured up and the boarding in place. I was hammering away when I found a crack in the inside plaster, so I peeped through at Elisabeth. Then I put my mouth near the crack.

"Peep-bo! I see you!" I had the mean pleasure of watching her jump and look round.

"Don't do that!" she called. "Now look what you've made me do!"

My little prank had so startled her that she had smeared emulsion paint across the wallpaper we'd put at the end wall for contrast. I couldn't say sorry through the wall in case I caused another involuntary reaction. She was, in fact, getting on very nicely with the paint roller. Later on I tried it myself, but it was useless on the uneven weather boarding, so I went back to my large brush. That night the electric cooker's internals blew up in the middle of cooking our supper. When our jarred nerves had recovered, we finished cooking on the camping Gaz stove we always kept in the boot of the car. On our next weekend there we managed to get a nearly new secondhand cooker in an electrical shop down a back street in Bradham. An obliging electrician brought it out, got the key off the Pettigrews who kept a spare for us, and installed it.

All that weekend, Gehenna-like, a fire burned unceasingly at the end of the garden, fed at intervals with worn-out carpets, bedding, and clothes. The smoke blowing over us towards the sea symbolized the last sad dispersal of somebody's life's baggage. Anything of use we took back with us to give to the charity shops. With thoughts of small, sandy feet to come, we fitted sturdy hair cord to the lounge and bedroom floors and tough vinyl squares to the kitchen and bathroom. Next came a small fridge and a stainless steel sink unit. Adding the phenomenal price of wood and paint to the total, we began to have little hope of seeing much change from spending a thousand pounds. China and cutlery and the odd pots and pans we mostly had involuntarily bequeathed to us by Mrs. Winscale. We added some "cheap and cheerful" items from Woolworth's, replaceable if guests broke them.

That night as we reluctantly left the fireside for bed, I mumbled to Elisabeth, "I suppose we ought to think about installing a phone."

"Oh, do we *have* to have one? It's such bliss to get away from it."

"Well, you know what happened last time when Charles was away from the office and Fred went down with flu." That was something we were not likely to forget. Charles couldn't be contacted; I wasn't feeling too good myself, and I just managed to hold the practice together working night and day. Afterward we all agreed—never again! When someone went on holiday, he would leave a number where he could be contacted.

"It'll have to be a coin-box one," I said. "Otherwise if any of your young relatives stay in the place, we shall probably be ruined."

Elisabeth sat up smartly. "Just because all your predatory relatives are in Canada or New Zealand."

"Sorry, I didn't really mean it. Still, all things considered, a coin-box it'll have to be."

Mentally I stuck "phone" on my list and watched our allocated thousand pounds shrinking to the vanishing point. Then I drifted off into merciful slumber.

While we were seated at breakfast, the sound of a powerful engine came in through the open window. Elisabeth craned her neck to see.

"It's a huge tractor coming down the field from the harbor end. Oh no! It's pulling a plow; they're plowing up our lovely field."

I was angry. Often we would see a covey of partridges pecking around near the sheep in that wide grassy stretch. Occasionally someone would come along the road, and then they would take off in a body and settle farther away.

The next time I saw Bert, he told us that the farmer was putting in a late crop of wheat.

"Don't know why he's doing it; there's enough wheat around in the country already."

"I wish he'd left it; we *did* enjoy that field," said Elisabeth.

"That's not all he's up to," Bert went on. "D'you know he's got a shooting butt down near the border of the bird sanctuary, and he brings his friends down at weekends in the season, and they blast off at the ducks coming in to the pond there. We have complained to the Nature Conservancy, but it seems he's within the law. I'd like to blast *him*—in the pants!" This was strong stuff coming from the amiable Bert, but he was one of the honorary wardens of the sanctuary. He did an annual Tern Watch, keeping an eye out for stray dogs or foxes that might harass the terns sitting on their eggs on the tiny shingle scrapes or feeding their infant mobile balls of down which were almost indistinguishable from the stones until they ran.

✛

Back in the practice at Wilverton, we watched winter creep by with its rain, snow, fog, and frosts, the monumental surgeries and never-ending visiting lists. I had been visiting Mrs. Fairbairn in the Duke of Gloucester Hospital whenever I could. For the first few days she had had a stormy passage. The fluid round her lung had turned out to be an empyema—infected matter. But after this crucial period, she began slowly to mend. It was a week or so later before I had time to look in again. When I asked the sister if I could see her, she smiled.

"You'll get a nice surprise, Doctor. Mrs. Fairbairn's our pride and joy! Do you know, now she's up and about she spends most of her time going round the lonely, elderly patients who don't get many visits, cheering them up and doing little acts of kindness for them, especially any who are distressed and needing someone just to sit by them. You know, *we* just don't have the time. She'll be discharged soon—we'll miss her. Got any more like her to send in?"

Mrs. Fairbairn was glad to see me, and I promised to visit her at home when she was discharged. When I did manage the call, the niece who lived with her had left the door on the latch for me. I went straight in. Mrs. Fairbairn was sitting in a comfy chair by a bright fire. As I entered, she quickly tucked something in tissue paper behind the cushion at her back.

She told me she was feeling wobbly but a lot better. The ambulance was calling next day to take her for a checkup at the hospital. "Then they're going to discharge me, I hope. I'm ever so grateful, Doctor, to them all, but 'specially to you. What you said when I had to go in just stuck with me. I've learned to rest—in God's arms. And I've got a verse for you; I read it in the Gideon Bible in my locker. Here it is. She opened her own Bible at a marker and read, "I will never leave you or forsake you. . . ."

We prayed together, and when I rose to go, she fumbled under her cushion and brought out the tissue-papered bundle and handed it to me. "When I was on the mend, I had lots of time." (It hadn't looked like that to me, seeing her buzzing round the ward on her

47

errands of mercy.) "So I'd like you to have this too." It was another pullover in a quiet lovat shade of wool.

At last with the first signs of spring, things seemed to dwindle down to the normal mad rush, and our thoughts began to turn with the lengthening days lightly to—Seascape. There it stood, ready, rebuilt, repainted, re-equipped and—blissfully, remote—just awaiting re-habitation. I begged an early week's holiday, pleading danger of imminent collapse. The partners looked at me in indulgent disbelief and told me to push off before they changed their minds. They hadn't forgotten completely that they had both had a week off after Christmas one after another, while I had borne the burden and the cold of the day, so to speak.

We didn't stop to argue but took off for the styx with indecent haste, just in case they did change their minds or some appalling emergency arose. It was the coldest April for many a year. Nevertheless we determined to make the most of the break, and we even had the heartless effrontery to ring the partners up on the second day to make solicitous inquiries as to the state of the practice. I could almost feel the steam rising at their end of the phone.

We garbed ourselves in anoraks and layers of sweaters and stalked daily along the beach for miles and miles watching the overwintering birds, safe in the knowledge that when we returned to the cottage, there would be a cheerful driftwood fire waiting and cups of coffee to be had in minutes.

Bert dropped in while we were finishing our breakfast on the second day. "Care to come over tonight for coffee? I promise you it *will* be the real thing, that caffeine-impregnated stuff you insist on drinking. We want you to meet some new neighbors of ours. You'll like them—they're an interesting couple, just retired here to live in the cottage they acquired a while back. They've become real friends of ours. You will come?"

"Thank you, we'll be there—about half-past seven," said Elisabeth.

The last glow faded from the sky as we made our way to the Pettigrews. Out to sea we saw the lights of a liner and a glimmer from one or two fishing boats far out on their way to their grounds. I watched one until its light passed out of sight. I thought I detected the dark shape of a small boat out near the point where the cliffs ran down to the water. It could have just been a trick of the light, so I dismissed it and walked quickly after Elisabeth.

Jean met us at the door and took us in to the sitting room. A cheerful, red-faced man rose to greet us while his white-haired wife smiled up at us from the sofa. I had an odd feeling that I knew her face, and I thought she looked rather attentively at mine. "Elisabeth, Andy, let me introduce Jenny and Fred Ire." Bert turned to the pair. "This is Elisabeth and Andy Hamilton."

We'd only been chatting for a few moments when Mrs. Ire asked me in sotto voce, "Forgive my asking you, Doctor, but didn't you train at King's College Hospital during the war?"

The penny suddenly dropped. Throwing etiquette to the winds, I grabbed her hands. "Nurse Jenny! Staff Nurse, Casualty, 1939! I knew I'd seen you somewhere before—well I'm blowed!" Then I realized that all the others, Elisabeth in particular, were staring at me.

"Sorry, everybody; I just recalled that Jenny and I were both at King's during the war and in the casualty where she was second in charge of the nursing and I was a raw medical student. Apart from being a bit superior *and* very nice-looking, she did manage to teach me quite a bit about patient care, and I was always grateful. I was a badly behaved student and was always ragging about, but I wasn't half as bad as Higgs, the Casualty Officer. Do you remember, Jenny, when he pushed Sister into a barrel and cut off her fringe with a pair of surgical scissors? You know that she forgave him and married him in the end?"

As the evening progressed, we found that these reminiscences had fairly set Fred off, and he turned out to be just as big a wag as old Higgs had been. As we left, I said to Bert at the door, "Sorry, Bert, I'm afraid we rather held the floor, and we were *your* guests, after all."

"Think nothing of it, Doc. It was so good seeing you all enjoying yourselves."

Even so, Elisabeth gave me quite a wigging on the way home about my bad manners. I wondered if she was just a teeny-weeny bit put out by the revelations of our frolics with the nursing staff in our youth. But she had found a lot in common with the Ires in the problems they had had in bringing up their family in huge, damp, old vicarages. Elisabeth knew all about those grim habitations of the country clergy.

It was pitch black on the path home. We could only see about twenty yards ahead.

"You know, Jenny has asked us to tea tomorrow? I said we'd love to come. Is that okay?" I nodded.

Elisabeth is usually a bit shy about going out to people we hardly know; I guessed that Fred had put her at ease with his memories of vicarage life.

Next day drizzle made outside painting out of the question, so I helped Elisabeth paint the skirting boards. I couldn't do much harm there as I took around a sheet of cardboard to catch the drips. I always make the mistake of taking too much paint on the brush under the impression that I save time by having to dip less in the pot. By the time I get the paint spread out, I probably take longer, apart from the mess my fingers get into from the paint running down the handle. At four o'clock I wiped the brush on the edge of the tin for the last time, stuck it into a jar of spirit, and started rubbing my fingers with a rag soaked in the stuff.

"Come on, darling," called Elisabeth from the front door. "It's past four. We ought to be at the Ires'."

I dashed to the sink, squeezed some washing-up liquid on to my hands, and rinsed them under the tap.

"Pooh! You can't go like that. Your hands smell awful!"

I grunted, went back to the bathroom, and deliberately washed my hands again with Elisabeth's special lavender soap, and ran out to catch up with her.

Fred greeted us as the doorway as if we were doing him a special favor by visiting his humble dwelling. It wasn't all that humble. The rooms were beautifully repainted throughout, and he had built on an extension to the lounge which gave him a spacious room thirty feet long with windows at each end—the one looking seaward and the other out over the farm fields. He had taken the plaster boarding off the ceiling to expose the timbers, which gave an impression of added height. Outside, the air was cold and clammy, but the house was delightfully warm. The source of heat was a fine free-standing Scandinavian wood stove. "Cosy, isn't it? And it doesn't cost us a penny. It just burns wood, and we get that for free off the beach. A builder from our old parish sold it to me cheaply. It had belonged to a wealthy client who had installed oil-fired central heating and didn't want it any more. Nice bit of iron-work, don't you think?"

We sat drinking our tea and listening to Fred. As he rattled on, I was looking surreptitiously around at the walls. I'm no judge of art, but it did seem to me that the paintings were not half-bad work. There were six or seven all together, including one behind me which I took a quick look around at. Fred spotted me.

"Taking a look at my work?"

"Sorry, I *was* listening to what you were saying, but they caught my attention."

"What do you think of them?"

"Well, I really think they are very good, but why is there always a tombstone in them? Are you keen on tombstones?" It seemed a macabre preoccupation and not a bit like his jovial character. He smiled.

"Actually they are Celtic crosses, and I *am* keen on them! Jenny and I once did a holiday tour to hunt them out. We saw the first in Iona. Then we found them in

Yorkshire, Wales, Cornwall, and—well, everywhere that there are traces of Celtic Christianity. They seemed to have a beauty and significance all of their own—full of spiritual lessons. The unshakeable faith of the craftsmen in the meaning of the death and resurrection of Jesus, signified by the cross and the perfect circle of life surrounding its head. They had withstood the ravages of time—and the Vikings! When guests see them, they often ask about them, and it gives the opportunity to share the good news with them."

"Thanks for telling us, Fred. We feel the same about Jesus, but we haven't your talent for painting what He means. Being a doctor sometimes makes for different occasions to say something though."

The evening passed quickly, and we were just getting ready to leave when Fred put a hand on my arm. "It would be good to have a little prayer before you go," he said, as naturally as if he had offered me another cup of tea. Sitting there by his bargain stove, we closed our eyes, and Fred prayed a simple prayer just like having a chat with a friend. He thanked God for our new friendship; he prayed for the sick folk who came to me for help; he prayed for our children and for the neighbors along the Ridge, and he put us in God's care for the future and asked that we would all do our utmost to do what He wanted at all times. We went out into the night feeling like those adverts for ready-made porridge—full of an inner glow.

Outside the wind was biting now, but it had cleared the drizzle, and a bright gibbous moon had changed the sea to rippling silver beyond the gray border of the fields. I stared out towards the point. No sign of any boat there now; I decided that it *had* been an optical illusion.

On our way to the beach next morning, we saw Bert and Jean bent down weeding behind a screen of tamarisks. We didn't mean to disturb them, but Jean straightened her back and spotted us by the gate. They both came down to greet us, their hands black with soil.

"Well, you two, how did you get on with the Ires last night? Nice pair, aren't they? Are you coming for longer this summer now you've got a place of your own? If you are, it'll give you a chance to meet some more of our neighbors. There are some interesting characters among them. You remember you told us how you first came here and camped in the railway carriages right up at the end of the Ridge? Well, they've also got some new occupants— Harriet Grimshaw and her son, Desmond. She's a widow. Her husband died some years ago. She supports herself painting. Now *she's* a *real* artist, no disparagement to old Fred, but her pictures are really beautiful! You should get one for Seascape. That's if you can afford it. She does seascapes best, but she concentrates mostly on impressionist work. You can see some in the art shop in Bradham, but I think they mostly go to a gallery in London. Jean doesn't like 'em, but, poor old dear, she always was a bit of a Philistine!"

He grinned and ducked as she aimed a half-hearted swipe at his head. "As for that lad, Desmond, after doing quite well at school, he seems at a bit of a loose end now. Does odd jobs and that sort of thing.

They've got a couple of dogs. You'll see them when you come in the summer all right."

I didn't know quite what he meant by that, but he went on. "There are two other families who only come down in the summer. There's a brother and a sister; she was a missionary in the Far East. They've got those two big bungalows farther up towards the Grimshaws. They've both got lots of children. I'm sure they would love to team up with your grandchildren if you coincide. I think you've missed them up 'til now. They are the exceptions to just about everyone else who lives here—no dogs!"

The Cox'un

I t really *was* the "cold" light of day—our last day. A nip in the air convinced us to keep clear of the beach and take a walk in the comparative cosiness of the harbor. We hadn't yet had a good look around it, and there were one or two things we wanted to pick up at the little general store as well. The tide was dropping, and the Bradey River was running swiftly through a narrow channel in the middle with several yards of mud on either side. On this rested about a dozen fishing boats and yachts, mooring ropes tight so that they did not heel over too much. The fish had been already unloaded in the early morning, packed, and dispatched far and wide. It would have been mostly cod, plaice, sole, mackerel, and "Robin Huss"—a local euphemism for dogfish.

We walked idly down to the lifeboat house standing with its slipway sticking out into the river beyond the mud—so that the boat could be launched at any state of the tide. We peeped through the open side door. In a little partitioned-off area sat a man, capless but in uniform, smoking a pipe and poring over papers on a desk, a telephone near his hand. He looked up and saw us against the light as we stood staring at the hull of the lifeboat towering above us on its cradle, its bows pointing to the big doors.

"Mornin'. Havin' a look around?" he asked in a friendly way.

"I don't suppose we could see over the boat?" I asked.

"Course you could; it's all part of my job; get's people interested, and then they are more ready to support the R.N.L.I. Come this way."

He led us to a wooden ramp up against the side of the stern where we could walk up steps to the wheelhouse.

"Where be to, sir? Visitors?" There was the unmistakable Cornish flavor to his speech. I was *sure* he wasn't a Sussex man.

"Yes, we're on holiday. We live along the coast at Wilverton, but we have a small bungalow on the Ridge."

"Glad to meet you. The name's Len Trevithic. I'm the Cox'un of the Bradham Harbor boat here."

That settled it; he was Cornish all right. As a boy I had spent many holidays in Cornwall.

"Pardon my asking, but aren't you a Cornishman? How is it that you're here in Sussex as the Cox of a lifeboat?"

"You're right, I'm a Newlyn man. It was the failure of the fishin'—pilchards and mackerel mostly—and too many foreign boats now. I managed to get started again here and then went over to this job after doing my time as a member of the crew."

I thought he must be a man of considerable personality to be so accepted amongst these conservative locals. He had dark curly hair going gray and small, piercing blue eyes and a sailor's brown, weather-beaten face. I felt I wouldn't have minded going to sea with a man like this in command.

There was just room for the three of us in the wheelhouse with the central wheel and a bank of controls before us. Below the windscreen was a round radar scanner. Trevithic gave us a steady stream of information about the capabilities of the boat to handle distress calls from ships in trouble. Afterward as we walked out, we saw photographs all round the walls of coxswains and crews going back a hundred and fifty years who had been instrumental in saving hundreds of lives. Maybe Trevithic had done his share, but he had omitted to tell us about that.

As we walked slowly back from the general store with our bits and pieces of grocery, Elisabeth said quietly, "You know, as he was showing us around, I couldn't help thinking of folk who've made a wreck of their lives. Jesus is like the Coxswain of the lifeboat. He sends out a call, and we should all come running to help, like those crew members, but I think we're often not listening. So He takes the others who get there first. He can save folk, but He needs our help."

That afternoon on the road back to Wilverton I thought about the future. I looked across at Elisabeth who seemed to be thinking things over herself.

"Well, what do you know? We have some interesting neighbors—a retired parson who paints tomb-stones for a hobby, and a wife acquainted with my murky past, an impressionist artist and her drop-out son, a pair of fanatical gardeners, and a horde of dogs. The mind boggles! It should be an interesting summer holiday this year!"

All the Birds of the Air

It was the middle of August, and the surgery was very warm. We had had the usual influx of holiday-makers with their temporary resident cards—people who had not brought enough of their regular pills to see them through 'til they got home, diabetics who had got off their regular diet without adjusting their insulin dosage, people with tummy upsets, people who had tried to get a suntan in two days, and some *real* emergencies. But the regulars were having their holidays too elsewhere, and so the pace of the work was about normal even though both of my partners were away.

I pressed the buzzer wearily, and in came Jos Blagdon. Now Jos was an old friend, a real Romany Gypsy, who now lived a stationary existence in his caravan behind some houses on the outskirts of

Wilverton. I perked up, for I had a soft spot for Mr. Blagdon.

"Hullo, Jos. How are you?" I stretched out a hand. He took it in his own horny one.

"Not so bad, thanks; 'ow're you? Didn't think I'd get you today, Doc," he went on. "Ain't yer going on no 'oliday this year then?"

I didn't reply to him at first, but I gave him the once-over and tested the urine specimen he had obediently brought. Only then I said, "You came just in time, Jos. I'm going away at the end of next week. We've got a little place at Bradham Harbor now, and we'll be away for a whole month. But mind you come for your next follow-up. You'll see Dr. McBride or Dr. Campbell."

He nodded reluctantly. "Ever been to Bradham fair, Doc? Lots of me pals from down in Kent an' Sussex an' as far as 'ampshire an' Surrey'll be there. The molishas'll be sellin' their baskets an' their flukes made outer shavin's, but the real fing to see is the greis—that's what it's all abaht—sellin' the greis. But you won't see no vaados there. Well, maybe one or two you might, but most on 'em come in their motor caravans these days, trailin' their 'orse boxes."

He made a face and waggled his head and shoulders to indicate how posh they'd all become. "Some of the locals walk over their greis; you watch out, Doc, an' see 'em runnin' 'em up and down, showin' 'em orf. An' you watch out for them mongers. There'll be a few arter yer cams, most on 'em diddycoys any way. They had a real good fair too, swings, roundabouts, and I bet there's some molt askin' to dukker for yer. You wanter go along with yer missus."

Because I'd picked up a few words of Romany, painfully I worked out that there would be horse dealers showing off their animals, Gypsy women selling baskets and artificial flowers made from shavings, beggars after my money (cams), Gypsy hangers-on (diddycoys), and women fortune-tellers. I was interested in Romany because the language has some origins in Sanskrit, for example, in such words as *char* for tea, and I found it fascinating that this linked with *chai* in Swahili, as that language has Indian origins too. Of course as the Gypsies passed in their wanderings through the Middle East and Europe, words from many languages had become incorporated into their vocabulary.

Jos went on. "But if you wanter see them showin' off the greis, yer gotta go early on." He wagged his head. "Wish I was a'comin', Doc. Allus useter in the old days; bit far now, but *you* go, an' you can tell me all abaht it afterwards," he finished wistfully.

I decided we'd try, just to please old Jos. Years before, he had come to my rescue when our caravan trailer had broken down away from home. He'd come out miles with his old horse and cart right over the South Downs and brought me a stub-axle and fitted it.

✝

The house at the harbor had already been put to good use. A missionary couple, impecunious as they always are, had had the use of it for a couple of weeks.

That suited us very well, for it kept it occupied and lessened the risks from squatters and vandalism. Our son Peter and his family would be coming to liven the place up for a week while we were there, and maybe our other offspring might turn up for a day or two as well. We were looking forward to it, bracing ourselves, and getting into mental training, as you might say, for the onslaught.

The morning after we arrived, we were peacefully sitting having our breakfast on the porch. It was rather late, for we had slept in a bit following all the packing, traveling, and unpacking. Without warning, a fusillade of barking rent the air, coming from up the road where the Ires lived. Among the doggy devotees of the Ridge, Fred and Jenny had an elderly, crotchety dachshund who spent most of his time in a basket. Something had got on his wick. Seconds later, past our gate loped a huge gray Irish wolfhound. He was followed by a middle-aged woman on a bicycle, then by a lad of about eighteen, also on a bicycle, and behind him another slightly smaller wolfhound.

They passed us in silence, but a moment later the Pettigrews' bull terrier gave tongue. When he cooled off a bit, his voice was joined by a series of high-pitched yelps which must have come from the Fergusons' Jack Russell, and then *he* was quickly followed by an angry yapping.

"That'll be that 'orrible little Scottie of the Billinghursts," I said. This contribution concluded the canine concerto. We waited for a couple of minutes or so, and, sure enough, we saw the Grimshaws, mother and son, for we were now sure they were none other, cycling along the causeway to the sea.

"Bert might have warned us that you could be savaged by a pair of rapacious wolfhounds if you walked abroad at this hour of day," I said plaintively.

"Don't be silly, darling. I guarantee they're only a couple of big softies. These highly bred specimens usually are."

"I wouldn't like to bet on it!" I grunted, for those great shaggy brutes looked like regular man-eaters.

"Anybody at home?" Bert Pettigrew stood on the porch.

"Hello, we've just seen an amazing sight . . ." I began.

"Oh, you mean the Grimshaws." Bert gave a short laugh. "Well, that happens regularly twice a day in the summer. You can tell the time by it."

"Those dogs looked pretty ferocious to me," I said.

"You don't have to worry. They come and put their paws on your shoulders and try to lick your face if they get half a chance. Still I wouldn't threaten Harriet or Des, not unless I wanted to lose a hand!"

I felt that Elisabeth and I were about equal in estimating dog ferocity, so I didn't pursue the matter further.

"I'm just going down to the village," said Bert. "Can I get you anything?"

"Thanks, but we were going ourselves. We have nothing for tea. I don't suppose there is a fish shop we haven't noticed?"

"No, but I tell you what—have you seen that pottery place? Well, the potter, bit of an odd chap he is, but one of the oddest things about him is that as well as selling pots, he sells lobsters. He's got some pots, the lobster variety, out in the bay near the cliffs where the rocks run out under the surface, and he does quite well with them. You might get a lobster off him if he hasn't sold out or taken them into Bradham Fish Shop already. One of those would make a nice tea."

"Thanks, we'll try that. We'd like to look at his pottery too."

Bert said, "Don't be put off by his manner. He is an odd bloke, as I say, but his lobsters are fine, all cooked on the premises, straight out of the sea."

Bert was right; when we went into the pottery place, Mr. Loader, the potter, looked as if he couldn't care whether we bought anything or not. We almost felt like intruders.

"I understand you sell lobsters," I said, almost apologetically. He jerked up his chin as a reply. "Could we have one, please?"

Without a word, he went into the storeroom at the back of the shop, opened a large refrigerator, and produced a lobster. It looked freshly cooked. He didn't overcharge, and when we had our lobster safe in a plastic bag, we stayed and looked around at the pots and pottery figures in the tiny shop.

He was clearly a skilled potter. There were some very fine jugs, plates, and mugs with pleasant fired-in decorations, mostly of wild flowers such as you could see on the marshes all round. Then we saw some other artifacts on one side. They were of local birds, animals, and fish—even a lobster on a flat rock waving its claws—all beautifully lifelike, but we noted with growing dismay what seemed to be the potter's almost sadistic delight in his treatment of his subjects. A mallard struggled, one leg seized by a nasty-looking pike. A stoat held a rabbit by the throat. You could see the terror in the rabbit's eyes. The least offensive was a coypu, the huge South American rodent with yellow teeth. These coypu had been imported by breeders for their "Nutria" fur, and they had escaped during the war and colonized parts of the Norfolk Broads where their burrowing had weakened the banks of many dikes. We had heard that some had been observed in the marshes of Southern England too. It was engaged harmlessly enough in eating the green shoot of a reed. We went outside.

"His work shows skill and brilliant realism, but there is something really cruel about it," I commented.

"He gives me the creeps," responded Elisabeth.

Nevertheless, the lobster, with a bit of cucumber and lettuce, went down a treat that night. I had bought a newspaper, and after supper we shared it out. It was the *Daily Express*, as they'd sold out of *Telegraphs*. There was a lurid story of kids on drugs in the metropolis. The police felt the supply route could be somewhere on the south coast, so the reporter said.

"Only guesswork," I observed. "If they had got a lead, the police wouldn't go telling the newspapers and give the blighters warning. I bet its slipping through airport customs somewhere."

The Grimshaws must have altered their normal schedule for that day; they did not come by in convoy that evening, but about an hour before dark, young

Desmond went by on his own, a haversack on his back. We saw him cycling over the causeway and along the sea wall westwards. Then he disappeared. It was almost dark when he passed by again on his way home. His haversack looked even more bulky than when he'd gone by the first time.

A few evenings later we were sitting, replete and happy, in the long sun room facing the sea. As we watched the flocks of gulls flying in for the night under the reddening sky, we heard the sound of tires on gravel. Desmond flew past, pack on back, down the track, over the causeway, and along the sea wall until again he disappeared from view.

"What can that lad be doing at this time in the evening?" wondered Elisabeth.

"Blessed if I know."

We turned in and didn't see or hear him return. I woke at 3:15. Whether it was a dream or what, I couldn't make up my mind, but as I lay there, a most ridiculous thought had come into my head. At intervals throughout the previous day I had thought about that newspaper report about drugs. *Could* it be? Could this lad's curious visits to the deserted part of the beach *possibly* have anything to do with it? A pick-up point? Ridiculous! And yet . . . I had been involved once before with a case of drug-running almost as unlikely. No! I turned over and put it out of my mind. In the morning when I remembered it in the cold light of day, it seemed just too absurd.

All the Fun of the Fair

Elisabeth was stirring the porridge while I laid the table. I called through, "You know we'll have to go to that fair today if I'm going to be able to tell old Jos Blagdon about it when we get back. He'll be disappointed if we haven't even made an effort. Let's go for just a couple of hours this afternoon. You could get in some riding on the horses."

At half-past two we parked our car in a by-road near the field outside Bradham. The jolly music was only recorded from a cinema organ, not the real thing from an old steam pipe organ, but it set our nostalgic centers humming.

I was disappointed to find that the horse sales were over. "Shan't be able to tell old Jos about the 'greis' after all, but let's look round anyway."

The fair was taking up most of a five-acre field—

swings, roundabouts, dodgems, a terrible machine called a whip which flung you round a ring sitting sideways, and sideshows galore. I found I had not lost all my throwing skill and succeeded in knocking off one coconut for Elisabeth. Then we wandered up to the roundabout.

"Come on, let's have a whirl!"

Elisabeth looked doubtful, but when it slowed to a halt, I persuaded her to mount one of the chargers while I got on another beside her. The music started, and we slowly gathered speed. On the row in front I saw a village lad sitting beside his girlfriend, nonchalantly refusing to hold on while he lit a cigarette. The man came around for our money, balancing himself to counteract the centrifugal force throwing him outwards. When he came to us, I saw to my surprise that it was Desmond. We knew each other by sight now, and he smiled.

"Doing this for a bit of spare cash," he said. As he went on forward to the couple ahead, I noticed the lad lean a little backwards to get his money out of his trouser pocket. Then it happened. He lost his balance, swayed uncontrollably back, grabbed for the brass pole, missed it, and with a yell, pitched over backwards, bouncing once on the wooden steps of the roundabout before he crashed into the spectators. Round we went again, but Desmond signaled the operator to stop. As we slowed, he leaped nimbly off and bent over a body on the ground. Then he stood up, waving the crowd back. A moment later I jumped off too. There was the young capsized rider, now on his feet and looking foolish and shaken. On the ground lay an old man, obviously in pain and unable to move.

The Bradham Harbor grapevine must have been in good working order because young Desmond knew my status. "Would you please take a look at this gentleman, Doctor?"

I knelt down beside the old man. He was conscious, but his lined face was drawn with shock and pain. "Where does it hurt you, old chap?" I asked quietly.

He didn't answer but feebly placed a hand over his left hip. I put a very gentle pressure over the joint (with the flat of my hand). He gave a little cry through his clenched teeth. Again I waved the spectators back, knelt again, and compared the length of his legs by examining the levels of each of his boot heels. Yes, the left heel was raised at least an inch. I bent over the injured man. "You are going to be all right. I am a doctor. You have damaged your left hip. We will get an ambulance, and they'll soon have you nice and warm and cared for in the hospital."

He nodded feebly with the ghost of a grateful smile. I stood up and spoke softly to Desmond. "I'm pretty certain his leg is broken below the hip joint. We must get an ambulance and have him into the hospital, but until it arrives, he is not to be moved. Can you get some blankets to put over him? Where is a telephone?"

"There's a phone box just outside the gate of the field," said one of the bystanders. I ran at once and found it.

It was just under fifteen minutes before we heard

the siren, and the ambulance, blue light flashing, swerved in through the gate. Directed enthusiastically by the bystanders, it wove its way across the field between the amusements, machines, and stalls to halt about ten yards away. They loaded the old man into the vehicle, had me put my diagnosis on an official form, and pulled away, siren going and light flashing.

I looked round and realized that the young man who had caused the disaster was not to be seen, nor his girlfriend either. I suspected he had quietly melted into the crowd now dispersing. But I was not allowed to go. The fair manager requested an eyewitness, plus a medical statement about the accident, which I wrote and signed in his caravan.

"Thank *you*, sir. You see we can be 'eld liable for an accident involving one of our machines. This should see us to rights, but I'd like to get me 'ands on that young man 'oo, by all accounts, was a 'showin' off on the 'orses. But 'tain't no good tryin' to catch up with 'im. Probably cleared right orf now. But thanks for your timely 'elp, sir."

"You might say a good word to that lad who was taking the money. He did just the right thing when it was needed."

"Oh, young Des. 'E's just a givin' casual 'elp, but I will 'ave a word, as you say."

After all this, our enthusiasm was damped for further amusements. We wandered off and found ourselves amongst the large living caravans of the machine owners. Meandering along, we pictured the lives of those for whom these were home. We were nearing one van, larger and smarter than the rest, when the half-door in the side above the portable step opened, and a young man dressed in a dark suit and carrying a briefcase appeared. He was such an incongruous figure there on a fairground that I looked at him closely. Why, I was sure I knew that face! Of course, he would be grown up, taller and more strongly built now, but there was no doubt about it—it was Jamie McFee. He turned and, waving to the gray-haired Gypsy woman looking out over the half-door, began to walk away from us. I had the impression that he edged along rather furtively, glancing around occasionally as if he didn't want to be observed. Then he left the path that led directly to the gate of the field and veered off towards the amusement booths.

Elisabeth and I followed about thirty yards astern, wondering what this smart-looking "city gent" was up to. Finally he stopped by the very coconut shy where I had thrown successfully a short while before. He glanced round once more, put down his briefcase, and fished some money out of his pocket. Poor chap! His first two throws went completely wide, and the third went straight over the top of the enclosure. There was a yell of fury and a sound of breaking china. I was now dead certain—it must be Jamie! He pressed some money into the owner's hand, pointed over the top, then grabbed his case, and hastened off towards the gate. I had to run to catch up with him. He was just about to turn up the lane when I called, "Jamie."

He looked round apprehensively, then stopped, and said in astonished relief, "Docco! Thank goodness, it's you!" That "docco" took me right back to the

Bradham Harbor camp where that was my official title with the boys.

As we walked briskly down the lane, the sounds of strife swelled behind us from the direction of the coconut shy. Jamie smartened his pace even more.

"I don't know what you're doing here, Jamie. The last I heard of you, you were an articled clerk." He blushed.

"I can explain everything—that sounds like someone caught in the act, doesn't it?"

"Your aim doesn't seem to have improved, Jamie," I teased. He blushed again.

"Why don't you come and explain over a meal? We only live a mile or two away. You remember—Bradham Harbor? We've just acquired a holiday cottage there. Are you free for a little while?"

"Well, that's very kind of you. That *was* my last job for the day."

It wasn't really cold, but we lit the wood fire in the living room just for cheerfulness. Jamie and I made toast while Elisabeth laid the table. We had heard that as soon as he had left school, he had gone into a solicitor's office in East Grinstead, and that was the last we knew. Now he was a junior partner in a law firm practicing in Lewes.

"There's something much more important that I must tell you," he went on.

"I'm sure you remember, apart from my total lack of ball-sense, and you saw just now I haven't improved much," he added with a grin, "I was absolutely a nonstarter in Christian things. I expect you recall too that I never appeared to take in any of the teaching in the

Bible class. The only thing that ever really got through to me was the R.A.F. officer's talk at the camp. Do you remember it?"

I did, as clear as a bell. It had been a dramatic story. The officer had been one of the Battle of Britain pilots on his third call-out for the day, and it was in drizzly overcast conditions. A Messerschmitt escorting some German bombers had come up on him unexpectedly, shot him up, and partly destroyed his instrument panel with a burst of fire. At once taking avoiding action, he had climbed beyond the lower cloud layer, and then he realized that without instruments he was lost. He panicked. For all he knew he might be heading out over the Channel, and his fuel would soon run out. Without thinking about it he prayed, "Oh God, please help me." Then came a short break in the clouds. He could see the ground, and he knew he wasn't many miles from his base. All he had to do was turn and fly straight home.

Even though it wasn't much of a prayer, God had answered. Now the officer wanted to do the right thing and find out more about Him. He looked up the chaplain, who explained what God had done in a far greater way to rescue him, by sending His Son to die. The officer saw that the only thing he could do was hand over his life to Someone like that.

Jamie explained, "I didn't show anything at the time. I was just as 'okkard' as ever, I guess. Well, when I went to Lewes, I met this girl and wanted to take her out, but she said that unless I was a Christian, she wasn't interested. So I went with her to a church that was really alive. All the Bible class teaching and the

R.A.F. bloke's story came back to me. I knelt down in my room that night and told Jesus I'd been wrong, asked Him to forgive me, and invited Him into my life. What a change! For a bit I didn't know what had hit me. Life really took on a new meaning. I started in a ham-fisted way to help her in the junior group at the church, and Katie—that's the girl—she and I are engaged now."

"Jamie, that's the best news we've heard in a long time. We're so glad you've become a real Christian and that you're engaged. I hope we'll get to meet Katie sometime."

"You certainly will, and—will you both come to our wedding? It won't be until I'm a bit more established in the firm."

We nodded enthusiastically. "Well, now we're into your great news, you can tell us what you were doing in a Gypsy caravan *and* playing at coconut shies over here?"

He smiled. "I won't be betraying a confidence if I tell you it was over a will for old Benjie Boswell. He's the clan chief in this part of the world. Half the shows at that fairground are owned by relatives of his. He's a really fine old boy with a big white walrus moustache, and he looks very fit for his age, but he seems to think that his days are numbered. He wanted his will made. That's odd, for real Romanies don't make wills. It's usually all sorted out among the family, and they used to burn the caravan too in a sort of funeral rite, but I don't see them burning that expensive van! He's a lot better off than most, and I guess he didn't want any bickering over his possessions when he's gone.

His own wife is dead; that was his sister in the caravan. We got the whole thing sewn up."

"I bet he had your fee all agreed, and it was there on the mantelpiece under a jug or something," I said.

"You're dead right! How did you know?"

"I've Gypsy clients too. That's how they always pay me."

Jamie went on. "I'll tell you one thing though—he wanted to appear quite stoical about death, but I could tell he was afraid. I wished I could have told him about the peace Jesus brings, but I knew he wouldn't have taken it from me. Do you know a good parson round here who could help him?"

"Yes, I do. He'd be just the right man if he feels he could take it on, but he'd have to square it with the local vicar. This is not my friend's patch."

He had to go soon after that, and we watched together as his tail light disappeared down the track. Then Elisabeth said, "Were you meaning to ask Mr. Ire to go and see the old Gypsy?"

"Yes, I was; he'd be just the chap, not too young and brash. But the whole crowd will be moving on on Sunday, so he'd have to go tomorrow or not at all. Shall I give him a ring now?"

Fred Ire said he'd be very pleased to help, and it would be quite okay with the vicar. He would drop in on Mr. Boswell next morning. His only engagement was the morning service at the Bradham Harbor church on Sunday.

"We'll be there in force. We've got our elder son and his family coming for a week, arriving tomorrow," I said.

"Well, don't be surprised if your contingent just about doubles the congregation. The locals aren't good at attending in the summer, though we may have other visitors to swell the ranks."

When I sat down again, Elisabeth switched on the radio for the weather forecast and the seven o'clock news. The forecast wasn't too promising. " . . . strong southwesterly winds increasing to gale force over the weekend in the Channel by Sunday morning, rain at times, visibility poor . . ."

"Not so good, perhaps it will be better after that." We were early to bed that night, for we'd got our work cut out in the morning to get the place ready for the invasion. As we opened the bedroom window for fresh air, the sound of the sea getting up came clearly over the field where the corn was now standing waist-high.

"Not too good for the farmer either. The wind will flatten that lot, but I suppose they can still get it up without too much trouble with the combine." Before we turned out the light, we read a bit and in our prayers remembered "those in peril on the sea" and Jamie and the old Gypsy.

A Tall Ship

Next morning gray clouds chased one another across the sky. After days of dry weather, we were waiting for another "cloud," a dust cloud following a small estate car bringing Peter and Clare and the children. They did not like weekend traffic and would have started at dawn from their college staff cottage in the Midlands where Peter ran an outdoor education center. We knew they probably would not arrive before midmorning, but we couldn't help taking a peek out the windows from time to time, "just in case."

When we'd got the spare double bed made up, a camp bed for Jackie, who was three, and the cot we'd borrowed from the Pettigrews for Janie, aged thirteen months, I went outside to the shed to see if I could find some old rags for dusters. I was looking up to flick away a cobweb when I noticed a long object wrapped in sacking resting on the cross beams. Intrigued, I fetched the steps and got it down, covering myself with dust in the process. Before I unwrapped the sacking, I knew what it was—a bicycle. It was a lady's bike, an aged Raleigh, dating from the time when the back mudguards had strings of twisted twine from the edge to the hub to keep long skirts from getting caught in the wheel. Only a few strands now remained, hanging from the mudguard. The tires were flat, and the frame was rusty, but to my delight the chain still went stiffly round in the case, even though the oil inside the case must have been congealed almost solid. There was a celluloid tube pump still in its holder, and when I pulled and pushed it up and down, miraculously it worked. Someone must have used the bike not too long before, I decided, for when I tried to blow up the tires, they went up—and they stayed up!

"What *are* you doing, Andy? We haven't finished, and I need those dusters. They could be here at anytime. Do get a move on."

"Look what I've found!"

Elisabeth peered in. "Oh, Andy, just the job for Pete to get along to the hide in the early morning!"

"That's what I thought. Crumbs! Mrs. Winscale was a little lady, but I didn't think she was as small as all that."

"Will you leave it now 'til we've finished inside?"

When we'd got everything shipshape, I went outside again, cleaned out the chain case with some paraffin, put in some car oil, raised the saddle to its full extent, oiled the wheels, wiped the whole bike clean, and wheeled it out to the front.

"Just going to give it a trial run," I called to Elisabeth, who was standing on the porch. She shook her head despairingly. I knew what she was thinking. *Still a kid at heart.* I wobbled off down the track, my knees permanently bent and shoulders hunched like Quasimodo. Of course Bert had to be admiring his roses in the front just at that precise moment. He stared after me open-mouthed as I sped past on my mini-mount, looking for all the world like a giant on a fairy cycle. Then I caught my toe on a stone sticking up in the track and swerved violently into the next door hedge. Shamefaced, I walked the bike back.

"I see you've found Mrs. Winscale's old charger," said Bert, as I reached his garden. "Did her shopping on that years ago." There was indeed a misshapen bicycle basket still holding by mildewed straps to the handlebars.

"Thought it would do for Peter to get along the sea wall to the hide."

He nodded. "Just as well he isn't as big as you."

We were having a well-earned cuppa in the kitchen when we heard the crunch of tires on the gravel. Before we could put our cups in the sink and get to the door, which stood ajar, it was pushed open and in rushed a chubby little boy. "Allo, Ganny!" he shouted, clasping Elisabeth round the knee.

"Hello, darling." Elisabeth bent to kiss him.

"Ullo, Gampa!" I kissed him too. He pulled my mustache in return.

In came Clare with a pudgy, smiling little girl in her arms. "Hello, Mum. Hello, Dad. Lovely to see you."

Peter followed, weighed down by suitcases, a bag full of nappies, and a potty chair.

"Where do I put this lot?" he asked.

"In the bedroom through here." I took one of the suitcases off him and led the way. "I'm afraid it's a bit of a scrum for you, all in the one room."

"What a lovely little house," said Clare.

"You should have seen it last year before Mum and I got cracking," I grunted.

"I can imagine," she replied.

"You know David and Sarah and company are coming early next week? We'd planned for them to have our blow-up tent and the camping bivouac I used in Africa. They're both pretty waterproof, but I wouldn't like to risk it in this wind. It's going to get up more too, according to the forecast."

"I heard it on the car radio, Dad," Peter said. "We'll just have to scrum down in the house. It'll be okay. Worse things happen at sea."

The next morning, faithful to my promise, we all staggered in the wind to the Bradham Harbor church. Fred Ire had been almost right. We did nearly double the congregation, but there were some other brown-looking holiday-makers and a few fishermen, looking weather-beaten and uncomfortable in their suits. It was a pity, for Fred gave a jolly good sermon on "I was sick and you visited me." I didn't hear too much of it though. I was busy a lot of the time drawing funny men for Jackie on an old envelope, but I wondered if Fred's visit to Benjie Boswell had inspired him to preach on this topic. After the service, he filled me in.

"I found the old man quite easily. His sister was a little slow letting me in wearing my dog collar. I think that she felt her brother wasn't as bad as all that! Anyway he soon thawed out, and we had a very good chat. After a bit he said quite suddenly, 'Do you know, yer Rev'rence, wen I were a lad, I useter go and 'ear Gypsy Smith wen we went ter that big fair on Midsummer Common at Cambridge; he would be preachin' in a big tent wiv the vicar of the parish. Allus had a service for us Gypsies, 'e did. Made us feel the Lord loved us even though not many other people did. Niver forget 'im, I won't. But—I ain't lived a good life, yer Rev'rence.' His face got very overcast and he said, 'I done a lot chorin' in me time, an' I once nearly maured a moush in a barney in a kitchema. Nearly got took by the gavengro.' He grinned then, but went serious again and told me a lot more. He had given his wife a beating more than once, and he felt this, especially now she was gone."

I tried to explain the Romany to Fred. "I'm no expert, Fred, but I think roughly what he said was that he'd done a lot of stealing in his time, nearly killed a man in a pub brawl once, and just avoided arrest."

"Well, I told him that we had all done wrong, and no matter how bad we had been, what we had to do was to tell God about it. He was ready to forgive us, and that was why Jesus had come to take our sins on Himself when He died on the cross. I told him that if we believed it and welcomed Him into our hearts, everything would be made right between us. He seemed to grasp it. He said that was what Gypsy Smith used to say. I left him a modern New Testament, and he said his daughter would read it to him as she had had some schooling. I'm glad you asked me to go. I'll try to keep in touch with him through his daughter."

"Gypsy Smith! I remember him," said Elisabeth. "It was my dad who used to back him up. Midsummer Common was in his parish. I was only small, but I went to hear the old man. He was short and powerfully built, a wonderful speaker. He told marvelous stories, and he had a super caravan, not like the one at Bradham fair, but still clean and shining inside. I think it belonged to one of his family really, because he used to tour around speaking and staying in the camps."

On Monday it had stopped raining, and Peter and I managed a walk towards the bird hide. He was looking out to sea, but there was little to see except for a few black-back gulls wheeling over the water. Then he suddenly stuck his binoculars to his eyes and stared through them intently.

"Dad, look at that! There's a big yacht out there. Fancy, in this weather!"

The wind was *very* strong, gusting up to gale force, and we had to shelter behind a breakwater to stand up at all. I took the binoculars. There was indeed a yacht, a tall-masted vessel, bearing slowly towards us on a long starboard tack, close-hauled and heeling violently, its bows burying themselves deep in the waves. We took turns watching as it turned and went racing away sharply on the port tack, heeling even more steeply.

"Either the skipper of that boat is very courageous and experienced, or else he's just plain dotty, going out in a wind and sea like this," I said. We followed it until it was nearly invisible in the rain and spume. Then it turned once more and tacked out of sight round the headland.

"I wouldn't like to be sailing on the *Broads* in a wind like this, let alone the open sea," said Peter. "Do you remember, Dad, when Barney went as crew for that crazy guy to sail to Ireland from Falmouth, and they nearly went straight on into the Atlantic?"

"Do I! Your mom was worried stiff until we heard they'd made it, and then it was only because Barney spotted the southern tip of Ireland through the murk. She said a few things about the man whose boat it was, I can tell you."

That night the wind swept and roared round our little house as if it would take the roof off. On Tuesday we managed to get the weather forecast at 6 A.M. before Jackie came clambering into our bed. It said winds would subside a little during the day.

We were washing up the dishes in a leisurely fashion, and I almost dropped the plate I was drying. On the news we heard that Mr. Heath's yacht, *Morning Cloud*, had been wrecked off Shoreham the previous night, and two crew members had been drowned. I looked at the others. "It was that boat that Peter and I saw yesterday afternoon!"

Apparently *Morning Cloud* had been on its way to Cowes from Burnham on Crouch. Other yachts had turned back, but the skipper and the crew had felt it was safer to go on when the weather improved slightly round the Kent coast. One of the two men drowned was Mr. Heath's godson, Christopher Chadd. It seemed that freak waves swamped the boat, and the rest of the crew had taken to a lifeboat and came in at about half-past seven, completely exhausted.

"I never thought," said Peter sadly, "that when I said, 'worse things happen at sea,' it would come true, literally."

S.O.S.

Conditions improved on Wednesday. We were expecting David and Sarah, so Peter and I decided to get the tents up in the back garden. Being mostly shingle, the ground was almost dried out. We pumped up the tubes of the blow-up tent's frame and pegged down the fly sheet over the top. Next we erected my safari tent—one of the neatest little jobs I ever saw. It could sleep two at a pinch and the blow-up three or four, if they were not too bulky. Little Jackie trotted around "helping." We had just finished when they all arrived.

It was still too cloudy for an afternoon on the beach, so we took biscuits and a thermos of tea and drove inland in convoy to a country station where they had revived an old steam train railway line. It was worth the trip just to see Jackie's face when he stood, round eyes, looking at a real live hissing "choo-choo." And his bliss knew no bounds when we all embarked for a short trip to the next station and back. We stopped on the way back by a medieval country church. I kept the children amused, but at a safe distance from it, by lighting the volcano kettle, and Elisabeth got the cups and biscuits ready while the others had a look at the church.

"Do you know, they've got a tooth of a mastodon at the back of the church. It's about six inches in width!" Peter, as usual, was on his zoological bent. Elisabeth and I had to go and view the dusty prehistoric molar, or whatever it was.

Next morning I pulled back the curtains about 6:30 and saw that at last a real August day was on the way. A twittering from swallows on the telegraph wires at the back came through the kitchen window when I went to make tea for the troops. Sadly, I realized the swallows were mustering for return to Africa.

When I took some tea in to Peter and Clare, I found she was on her own with the children. "Where's Pete?"

Clare opened one eye. "Gone off on the bike to the bird hide," she mumbled.

I was surprised she knew. "When Clare goes to bed," Pete had told us, "she doesn't go to sleep; she passes out and doesn't come to life again until breakfast time." She did manage today to sit up and take the cup of tea.

When I took Elisabeth hers, she told me she had just seen someone cycling madly back along the sea wall. "I bet it was Pete. He's gone out, hasn't he?"

"Yep, he'll be back for his tea in a minute."

Sure enough, moments later we heard him clattering by the window as he put the bike back in the shed. He came in with his eyes sparkling with excitement and with tears from the cold air.

"Guess what I've just seen! A marsh harrier! They're not rare here, but I can't remember seeing one before in all the years we've been coming. He was hovering just this side of the sea wall, and as he moved along, every time he stopped to observe the ground more closely, up came a flight of smaller birds to move him on. First of all some rooks dive-bombed him, and when he was off their patch, a bunch of starlings took over, and then a mass of sparrows came off the cornfield and buzzed him. In the end he gave up and went off over the marsh. It was just like a film drama. Another thing, I'm almost certain I saw an arctic tern amongst the common terns on the pool island."

"Well done—glad you saw something exciting. Would you like a cup of tea?"

It's hard going out with Pete. Every minute you're stopping to look at some bug or flower. He spots things that I need a magnifying glass to see. The only time I got one up on him was when I spotted a red-breasted merganser duck on Lake Vyrnwy in North Wales before he did. Even then I didn't know the name of the bird until he told me.

It was that pleasant moment in the day when you push back your chairs from the table, or like some of the less well-trained members, rest your elbows on the table, and comfortably contemplate the day with bon homie. That pause in the conversation was shattered by a "poop-poop-peep-poop," and there on the track was Barney in his small battered open-topped Triumph (fitted with its totally incongruous Rolls

Royce three-toned horn), and sitting beside him a dark-eyed, brown-haired, laughing girl.

"Yoo-hoo!" Barney greeted us respectfully. He introduced to us his slightly shy girlfriend.

"Are you staying the night?" asked Elisabeth with mixed hope and apprehension (based on limited accommodation and food supplies and her joy at seeing Barney).

"Sorry, Mum. Judy's on duty tonight, and I've got an out-patient clinic at nine tomorrow—no can do."

"Would you like a picnic on the beach?" asked Elisabeth.

"Just the job," said Barney. "Okay by you, Judy?"

"I'd love it," she replied. "I haven't seen the sea for months."

This was good; our normal long-protracted argument about what we should do was nicely terminated, and all four ladies got cracking on the food while the men washed the dishes. We eventually proceeded beach-wards. There amazing sand castles grew from the spadework of the men and children. Enormous waterworks were created and destroyed.

Elisabeth and I meandered around the beach picking up shells to decorate the great sand edifices. Elisabeth concerned herself whether the children would (a) drown, (b) get sunburned or (c) decapitate one another with the spades.

Then it happened—not a decapitation, but a loud explosion from the direction of the harbor. I knew at once what it was.

"That's the call-out for the lifeboat. Anybody

want to go and see the launch? It's only about a quarter of a mile by the sea wall."

"I'll stay and help with the children if you want to go," offered David. "I'm not all that keen on lifeboats."

"I'll keep the kids amused too," said Barney.

"I'll come," said Peter. We got our shoes from the picnic spot and started down the sea wall at a fast walk. A little crowd of villagers and visitors had gathered by the lifeboat shed when we got there, and it looked as if the last crew members were just arriving. The coxswain was talking urgently to one of the older crewmen. There seemed to be a hitch. An old fisherman in a guernsey was standing in front of us.

I asked him, "What's the hold-up? Why don't they get off?"

He took the pipe out of his mouth and spat on the wharf. "Aren't no doctor turned up yet, I guess."

I turned round to Peter. "Look, I'll see if I can help. If they take me, will you tell Mum I'll be back soon."

He gave me a look which said, "Aren't you getting a bit old for this sort of caper?" But he just nodded.

I pushed through to where the cox was still talking to the crewmen. "You need a doctor? Could I be of any assistance? Of course, I haven't my medical kit with me."

I think that Trevithic was so concerned with the delay in launching that at first he did not recognize me. Then his grim expression softened. "Why, we met the other day! An' you a doctor too; well, we'll certainly take you if you're game. We've wasted enough time as it is, what with contacting Dr. Andrews. He's out on a maternity case, and his partner's on holiday.

Ye're really an answer to prayer. Sure ye want to come?" I nodded.

I looked round at Peter who was standing on tip-toe at the back of the crowd, waved to him, and signaled. I caught the look of resignation on his face and saw him shrug his shoulders as he watched me turn to follow Trevithic. We hurried into the lifeboat house and over to the hooks where all the crew's gear hung. He selected a pair of waterproof trousers and a jerkin.

"Here, Doctor, try these for size. They're Dr. Andrews's. He's a big man too, so they ought to fit." I put them on, plus a pair of sea boots, an inflatable life jacket, and a waterproof hat. We hurried up the ladder to the deck.

As we entered the wheelhouse, with the eight-man crew already waiting impatiently at their stations, Trevithic shouted an order, and we began to move forward. The winch attached to the bows towed us out to the top of the slipway, unhooked us, and down we went, gathering speed, to plunge deep into the mouth of the river. The engines throbbed, and the cox'un at the wheel swung the boat round seawards.

Trevithic handed over the wheel to his assistant. "We are dealing with an accident case on a Spanish refrigerator ship, the *Polstar*," he explained, "about three thousand tons, out of Alicante in southern Spain with a cargo of oranges, grapes, and tomatoes. The second mate was going down to inspect the cargo when he slipped on the stairway and hit a projecting steel rib of the ship. He was badly injured and needs urgent attention, they said. He is a very big man, and they are waiting until a doctor sees him before trying to move him." He added, "All the Spanish merchant navy captains have to be able to speak English so we have had quite a clear account."

"Was anything further said as to the exact nature of his injuries?"

"They can't be sure. He is unconscious so he can't tell them where he feels pain, but they reckon he has broken a leg and may have internal injuries as well. Ye've got a right job on your hands, Doctor."

I was apprehensive, but it was good to feel wanted. I listened to the continuous crackle of information coming over the intercom from the radio crewman, passing on directions and information from shore. We were making very good time, and Trevithic reckoned that if the sea remained calm, we should be alongside the *Polstar* within the hour.

I began to realize what tough fellows these lifeboatmen were. Today was fine, but even if it were as rough as on the day the *Morning Cloud* went down, they still would have been on deck, completely exposed to the elements and kept from being washed overboard only by their safety lines secured to various fixed points. The bowman was in the worst position, for with every downward plunge into the sea, he would be deluged with water. There *was* a canvas-covered hold forward and the wireless room aft, but apart from these, only the wheelhouse gave any shelter. Yet they cheerfully went about their tasks.

From the relative luxury of the wheelhouse I was really beginning to enjoy the trip with its sense of a unity of endeavor and spice of adventure. As we began our final approach, the cox took over the helm and brought us in a tight arc round to the leeward and calmer side of the ship. Small though it had at first appeared, the boat now towered above us, riding at anchor. Our crew were all on the alert, and when a rope ladder with wooden treads came snaking down the side of the ship, it was adroitly snared with a boat hook while other men were pushing out rope fenders and keeping us off as we closed with the *Polstar*. Our engines, which had slowed as the cox put us in reverse, were now just ticking over sufficiently to keep us in position.

"I'll go first," said the assistant cox, who had the emergency medical bag over his shoulder. "Then will you follow me, Doctor?"

He judged his moment, jumped for the ladder, and was soon up and over the side. I imitated him, grabbing at the swinging ladder and nearly missing my footing in the process. Climbing it wasn't as easy as it had looked, especially when the ship rolled slightly, and the ladder swung out from the side, but I made it up to the rails where a couple of strong hands hauled me safely on board. I was introduced to the captain, one Francesco Mico, and he took me to the top of an iron ladder leading down to the metal door into the refrigerated hold. I peered down. On the floor below a gigantic form was lying, chest downward with the head turned sideways, an admirably correct position for a badly injured man who might have his breathing obstructed if he had been lying on his back.

"He is hurt ver' bad, Doctor. We do not move him more."

I went down the ladder, and the seaman minding

the injured man stood back. The poor fellow was indeed badly hurt. He had a huge bruise and a cut on his temple. He was very pale, and he was breathing rapidly with difficulty. His pulse was fast and weak. Everything indicated that he was in severe shock. His left tibia and fibula were fractured, his foot lying out at an unnatural angle, and his blood pressure registered very low on the sphygmomanometer they had supplied me with. As far as I could tell, he had also a severe abdominal injury which, from his general condition, suggested to me a ruptured spleen bleeding into his peritoneum.

I went back on deck and let Trevithic know I wanted some splints and the Neil Robertson stretcher, a wonderful apparatus made of canvas and bamboo strips. When strapped around a patient, it cocoons him in a semi-rigid structure, enabling him to be moved like a parcel in almost any position. We put his broken leg in splints and then encased his body in the stretcher. The derrick lifted him to the deck. Then he was relifted, swung out over the side, and lowered to the lifeboat.

"The best place for him, Doctor, is on the floor of the wheelhouse behind us—much warmer and protected than in the forward hold, and it's too difficult trying to get a man this size into the engine room," shouted Trevithic.

"We'll settle him as comfortably as possible with his legs raised," I shouted back.

Captain Mico thanked me profusely and, to my embarrassment, kissed me on both cheeks under the interested eyes of our crew. We cast off. Our return journey was a little shorter than the one out, with the sea running in our favor, but as I hovered over the sick man in the cramped confines of the wheelhouse, it seemed longer. We kept his legs raised to counteract shock. I longed for some intravenous plasma. Thankfully his condition had not worsened.

I was bending over him to check his pulse when I heard the cox'un say at last, "Coming in now, Doctor. We're just in the river mouth."

We coasted slowly up to the runway, the helmsman judging it with great skill, and we were hooked on and slowly pulled up the slope. An ambulance stood waiting. It took six men to manhandle the injured man to the ground, strapped again in his stretcher, where willing hands got him into the ambulance. The driver gave me a look of recognition. He was the same one who had come to the Bradham fair accident. Off they went.

In the lifeboat shed where the boat, now turned to face the sea again, was undergoing a complete check of its gear, Trevithic shook my hand.

"Good work, Doctor. We are grateful to you. Dr. Andrews wouldn't have done better."

I walked slowly back along the sea wall and found the family on the watch for me, all agog to hear about Grandpa's trip in the lifeboat. I did my best to make a story out of it and asked them to pray for the sailor when they went to bed that night.

Poor Barney was wishing he had come with us now. I wished he had as well. He would have been much better at coping with the casualty, *and* he would have made a better job of jumping for the ladder to get aboard.

"That's the way the cookie crumbles," he commented with an assumed American accent.

"He jolly well kept the children happy," said Elisabeth, who was getting over being cross with me for taking risks at my age.

Judy gave him a quiet smile. I wondered what was brewing. Barney had had a bevy of girlfriends, but she was the best of them—by miles.

In the evening we rang the hospital, and the house surgeon told me that they had indeed found a ruptured spleen. The sailor's fracture had been reduced and plastered, and he was slowly returning to consciousness.

"Tough cookie, this señor!" was his comment, adding that their greatest trouble was going to be keeping him under control as he was not able to speak English and was built like a tank. I made a mental note to tell the children in the morning so that we could say thank-you to Jesus. I heard that two days later the sailor was sitting up in bed and demanding food in Spanish. He certainly *was* a tough cookie.

No Fire Without Smoke

An unnatural hush had fallen on Seascape. I dabbed moodily at a plate I was washing with a little plastic sponge on a stick. "You miss 'em when they're gone even though when they're around *all* the time, you long for a bit of peace." I rinsed the plate under the cold tap and stuck it in the drying rack.

After an early breakfast Peter and Clare and the children had set out for home. David and Sarah and company had gone the day before. We had told Peter to push off at once to try to avoid the congestion on the roads with all the late holiday-makers either going or coming. Things felt now definitely flat.

"Let's have a cup of tea on the grass. I don't feel like the beach just now."

I was negotiating the front steps with the tray when two successive explosions of barking commenced as the convoy of Irish wolfhounds and Grimshaws passed. I managed not to spill the tea and sat down in my deck chair to survey the scene with a slightly jaundiced eye. The jaundice deepened when the roar of an engine was followed moments later by the appearance of a giant combine harvester at the far end of the field near the nature reserve. It began cutting and combining the wheat, leaving the trail of short-stemmed straw in lines in its wake. Trundling beside it came an open, tanklike truck receiving the grain from the combine's chute. Steadily they circumnavigated the field. By the time they were coming down our side of the field again, the interest had worn off, and we decided in default of going to the beach to take a walk inland and have a look at a little wood between us and the Bradey River.

It was at that point that a little red van came dodging down the track and halted at our gate.

"Mornin', sir. Got a letter for you. You are Dr. Hamilton?"

The postman handed me the letter, put a finger to his cap, and went on.

"I wonder who is writing to us here." I looked at the handwriting. "I don't recognize this." I handed it to Elisabeth.

"Mmm—don't know it either," she said and then opened it and began reading. "Oh, this is nice! It's from Alison, you know, Jenny's daughter—Jenny, my classmate. Well, she says she's suddenly got this weekend free and wonders if she could possibly come for a visit. She'll ring us up this morning. Do you mind?"

"Of course not; I think I remember her now—a big, hearty, fair-haired girl, isn't she?"

We didn't have long to wait. When the telephone rang, Elisabeth answered it.

"Yes, quite okay, around four o'clock then. Fine, bye-bye."

There was plenty of time now for our walk, so we packed a few sandwiches and a flask of tea into a haversack and took off for the wood with our binoculars. With the reed beds near, it was a good place for edge and reed warblers, and we had heard a grasshopper warbler there as well one summer, though we never caught sight of it. Perhaps we would be luckier today.

Birdwatchers are not very gregarious, so we were a mite put out to find someone there before us. We just caught sight of a figure standing stock-still behind some bushes. We couldn't grumble. He obviously wasn't one of those bungling twitchers who crash through the undergrowth, frightening everything within earshot in their efforts to notch up another species. Then we heard that wonderful "churring" song again, really quite like an energetic grasshopper. But once again we couldn't spot it. Its churring stopped. Then quietly the other birdwatcher emerged from the bushes. It was Desmond Grimshaw! He had a fine pair of Zeiss binoculars hanging from his neck outside his camouflaged anorak. I could tell them yards off.

"Hello, we meet again," he said in a friendly way. "Did you see that grasshopper warbler?"

"No, we only heard it."

"It's pretty chancy. I've been waiting for about ten minutes, and I only saw it for a few seconds. Elusive little blighter."

We wandered through the bushes together. I noticed that he trod with great care, and yet he seemed to be looking everywhere at the same time as well. He was clearly an old hand. He was always seconds ahead of even Elisabeth in spotting a bird. She hears the song and then looks for the bird.

"I wonder if you would like to share our picnic? I'm sure we've got ample for three—only sandwiches, I'm afraid," Elisabeth invited.

"I'd love to—thanks."

We found a bit of level grass on the edge of a reedy dike and spread ourselves out.

"By the way, did you hear how that old boy at the fair got on?" he asked through a mouthful of ham and bread.

"I'm afraid not. You see, I'm not his regular doctor; the local chap would be the one to be informed."

I could see that his eyes were looking up into some trees on the edge of the wood.

"D'you see that thing up there?"

I followed his finger, screwing up my eyes . . . It couldn't be! "Looks to me like a lavatory seat!" I said.

"Right! People used to come and dump their rubbish here 'til one or two got heavy fines, and some idiot threw that up into the tree. But you'll never guess what I saw one evening when I was doing a bit of spotting! A tawny owl! There he was perched in it, just as if posing in a picture frame. I expect he found it a nice vantage point for looking for voles."

"Do you go down to the beach birdwatching in the evenings? I've seen you going by once or twice?" I asked him, feeling uneasy in the pit of my stomach.

"Yes, quite often. You see the birds coming inland from their foraging, and it's a good time for other things too—nice and quiet. I saw a pair of gray seals there once, not a hundred yards out towards the point. *And* if there's been a high tide during the day, you quite often can do a bit of useful beach-combing before anyone else gets there! I picked up a nice pair of brass-nozzled bellows once. The leather needed patching—that was all. I can't imagine who would drop such a thing overboard."

"Did you ever see a boat out there near the point?" I asked. "I thought I saw one, one night, but it could have been a shadow on the water."

"Well, of course, old Loader, the potter—he goes out there in his little outboard after his lobster pots, but you wouldn't see him there near dark. Can't say I've seen any other."

While he was talking, I'd come to a decision. This lad might be out of work. He might even be work-shy, but he was no drug smuggler. Not in a million years. I swallowed hard.

"Look, Desmond, may I call you that? I have an apology to make to you." He looked at me with surprise. I charged on. "When I saw you going by in the evening on several occasions, I got the crazy notion that you might somehow be mixed up in this drug-smuggling racket that the police say is being carried on over the south coast. I want to say I'm sorry for even having the thought."

He was staring at me open-mouthed as if he thought I had gone off my rocker. Then he laughed and laughed and laughed. When he'd recovered himself, he said, "Sorry about that. You see, I wouldn't get within miles of that stuff. There was a boy at school—in fact several boys—involved with drugs. Of course, they got caught in the end, and the worst boy was sent off to a remand home. Drugs! Not me!" His face grew serious. "But why did you tell me? You didn't have to!"

"Look, I'd had a rotten and unfounded suspicion about you. I'm a Christian, and I was wrong, and so I had to put it right even though you knew nothing about it."

He looked embarrassed. "Oh well, let's forget it."

We finished up our sandwiches and shared the tea. We still kept a lookout for any water birds while we relaxed after we had finished. All we saw was a coot sculling across the dike about twenty yards away and a vole who came out of his hole on the opposite bank to make a v-shaped ripple on the water as he hurried downstream on personal business.

"Andrew, it's getting on. We must go back. Alison might arrive earlier than she said."

We packed up and set off for home, and Desmond came with us. I was feeling a new sense of companionship with him now.

"What did you do in your 'A' Levels at school?" I asked.

"Biology, geography, and art."

"Any idea what you want to do now?"

He frowned and paused. Then it came out, almost

defiantly. "I'm going to be the warden of a wildlife center. I know I have to do a training, and I'm hoping to get accepted for one next year, but for the moment Mr. McBeath has agreed to let me help him as a more or less unpaid assistant. I start next week. My mother wanted me to go to art college, but I couldn't stick that. Indoors for three years and then trying to make some nasty little kids draw pictures when they don't want to! No thank you!"

Back at the bungalow we began preparing for Alison. Four o'clock went by, then half-past; then it was five to five. "I expect she's stuck in the traffic," said Elisabeth.

At five we heard a tremendous scrunch in the gravel, and Alison came tumbling out of a battered little coupe.

"I'm so sorry. I forgot the name of the house, and I stopped at a house beyond you. Some people called Ire; they were so kind I sort of got stuck there—sorry. Mrs. Ire said she had been a nurse at the hospital with you. Their son was there with them too. He's training for the ministry at a parson factory called Oakhill."

I wasn't sure if Frank Ire would have approved of this description of his son's theological college.

"The son's a great big bloke with a fair beard." She said this with studied carelessness, but I thought I detected a slight deepening of color in her rosy complexion.

Elisabeth is even more sensitive to atmosphere than I am, and this one seemed to have become moderately charged. "Perhaps we could ask him in for coffee or something. He must be the only young person around here—apart from a boy called Desmond up at the end of the road, but he's just a teenager."

Quickly Alison said, "Oh, I don't think I'd bother. He wants to see his folks, and anyway I came down to see you as well as get out of the smoke." She didn't fool either of us, but we dropped the subject.

On Saturday morning we went to the beach. Behind a breakwater Alison lost no time getting into a swim suit. She beat me to the sea, plunged in, and set off at a great pace as if she were going to swim the Channel. Elisabeth had a slight cold and didn't join in. When we got back to her, I set about getting my famous volcano kettle going. Alison dried herself and stood looking happily out to sea, her fair hair all tousled.

"This is marvelous, so lovely after London."

That night Elisabeth and I were talking quietly in bed.

"You know she's had a nasty knock quite recently? She was virtually engaged to a young house surgeon, and then he went to another job, broke it off, and married a woman doctor on the house with him. It would be nice if this young Ire could help take her mind off it."

After church on Sunday morning a huge young chap with a fair beard came out after us. He was at least six-feet-four and as broad as a door. He introduced himself as Graham Ire and walked back with us.

"Not a bad sermon from Dad today," he said breezily. Then he added more seriously, "If I can do half as well, I shan't mind." Alison smiled shyly at him. As he left us at the gate, he asked her, "You like a run out in my buggy this afternoon, Alison? Are you interested in old churches? There's one not far from here we could take a look at."

She looked inquiringly at us.

"Of course, you go, Alison dear. We can have a nice snooze!" Elisabeth made a pretty poor effort at concealing her delight.

"Thanks, I'd like to," said Alison.

"It's not that one with the prehistoric tooth, is it?" I asked.

"Oh, I know that one. No, it's another place where they've got some marvelous brasses. They're much better value than that old tooth."

Just after two o'clock, an M.G. sports car pulled up outside Seascape. Graham and Alison disappeared in a cloud of dust and spurting gravel, with Alison waving and looking radiant.

When they returned, Alison intently told us all about the brasses and the communal grave where a group of smugglers, all shot by excise men in the eighteenth century, lay buried. When she had gone to her room to spruce up, Elisabeth gave me a silent knowing look.

Early next morning after a hurried breakfast, she took off again, "back to the smoke." I went down to the store for some more provender. Alison was not only a big girl—she was a big eater, and we needed some restocking. I picked up a paper there. On the bottom of page three was another paragraph about the continuing supply of hash getting through to the pushers in London. The police were switching their investigations from the south coast to elsewhere.

As I walked back, a tractor towing a trailer stacked with baled straw passed me. Only one or two odd bales remained in the stubble the combine harvester had left behind.

✚

When we woke next day, it was to a beautiful cloudless sky. We had our morning tea, Bible reading, and prayer while sitting in the sunshine. I had just finished my prayer when Elisabeth grabbed my arm. "Look over there," she said.

I refrained from accusing her of having her eyes open during prayer and quietly fetched our binoculars. There on a bale of straw about a hundred yards across the field of stubble were a pair of fox cubs playing together. As we watched, an adult fox appeared from the dike and joined them, looking around with alertness. Then we heard it—the tractor coming down the lane and entering the gate. The foxes rapidly disappeared beneath the dike bank. The farmer stopped his tractor and came walking across the field with a shotgun over his shoulder. Behind him an old farm van disgorged two men and two black retrievers. The wind was blowing from the southwest. One of the men walked up to the west end of the field. The other whistled to the dogs, who began scouring the field. Just for a moment the big fox left the cover of the bank. When the farmer spotted him, he brought the shotgun up to his shoulder.

"Get down, foxy!" exclaimed Elisabeth. As if he had heard her, the wily Reynard disappeared under the bank edge again. We could almost hear the farmer's curses. The man with the dogs sent them tearing across the field to the dike. They were too late. A moment or two later the excited audience at Seascape saw the fox trio emerge well out of range, climb over the causeway with total nonchalance, and disappear into the oil seed rape on the other side. The farmer recalled the dogs and waved to the man at the west side of the field. He bent, picked up a handful of straw, and in a second we saw smoke rising from it as he threw it on to the small line the baler had failed to pick up. A ribbon of smoke and flame began its progress down the field, preceded by clouds of smoke. The fire-raiser now walked across the head of the field repeating the process, and soon a line of fire advanced with smoke sweeping on in huge billows. At the side of the fire stalked the farmer, gun ready in his hands.

Away ahead a cock pheasant sprang whirring off the ground. "Bang!" The beautiful bird fell, a bundle of ragged feathers. A whistle sounded, and one of the dogs raced to pick up the dead bird.

"That smoke is coming our way!" said Elisabeth. She was right. The wind had veered to the south, and we were becoming steadily more and more enveloped in it. Soon our side of the field was alight, and the flames were licking at the fence posts. A cloud of ash began to fall. The farmer hadn't bothered to plow a firebreak around the edge of the field, though the wind had increased and was now definitely more southerly. We retreated inside and shut all the doors and windows. Through the window we saw the fire moving inexorably onwards. It reached the causeway to the sea and burnt its way over with a burst of flame. On the other side a broad field dike full of water halted it. Only a few pieces of burning grass blew over, and the farm workers, now thoroughly alert to the dangers they had caused, began furiously to beat them out. We could just see their heads over the top of the dike as they flailed away with branches they had pulled off the scrubby bushes.

I glared out of the window. "Look at my car!" As the smoke cleared, I saw my once nicely polished car covered with a coating of white ash.

The phone rang. Bert's voice sounded uncharacteristically serious. "Doc, I'm sorry to bother you. Could you possibly look in and see Jean? You know she's had chest trouble on and off for years. Well, this smoke has upset her properly. She's very wheezy. I would be grateful. I know Dr. Andrews is on his own and very busy! I don't want to bother him. Perhaps if you could just see her and decide whether it's really necessary to get him out. Sorry, Doc."

"I'll be right round. Give me half a minute to get my bag from the car boot."

I found Jean in a bad asthmatic attack; she was breathing in quickly in short, forced gasps and then pushing air out in long wheezes. As I listened, I could hear that her chest was full of whining noises. She was very blue as she sat forward in a chair. I went into the kitchen, ostensibly to get something from my bag on the table.

"She's got a nasty asthma attack," I said to Bert.

"Yes, she's allergic to smoke. If we have a garden bonfire, she has to keep well away. She's tried her inhaler, but it doesn't seem to help much."

"No, and she mustn't use that too many times," I warned. "It can upset the heart. I've got some injections in my bag, but I'll have to contact Andrews before I do anything. Have you got his number?"

As expected, Dr. Andrews was up to his eyes with a surgery still half-full of patients. Yes, he would be immensely grateful if I could do some emergency treatment, and he would come out later. "Aren't you the chap who sent in the old fellow with a broken hip from the fair?" he asked. "Making you work, aren't we?"

"I'm just going to give you an injection. It will gradually relieve your breathing," I told Jean. I shot in a good dose of hydrocortisone. "It'll take a little time, but you should feel better soon, and Dr. Andrews will come and see you as soon as he's free." In between breaths Jean gave me a fleeting smile.

"I'm really grateful, Doc," said Bert in the little hallway, squeezing my arm.

The Lighthouse

I was standing shaving in front of the bathroom mirror next morning with the usual pleasant smell of frying bacon wafting in from the kitchen when Elisabeth called, "Do you know what I'd like to do today?"

"Go to the bird sanctuary again?" I hazarded.

"No, I'd love to see the Shambles Point Lighthouse. You can get shown round most days. Would you like to? We could take another picnic. They're sure to start plowing the field, and we don't want to get covered in ash and dust all over again. Better to go off somewhere for the day, don't you think?"

"Okay. I'll make the sandwiches."

I loved making sandwiches. I make 'em big and thick, and then if Elisabeth finds hers too much, she passes what's left on to me. These were going to be cheese and tomato.

✛

We had soon left Bradham Harbor behind and were crossing the bridge over the Bradey to set off across the marshes.

"I've always wanted to see Shambles Lighthouse ever since I saw it on that Christmas card. You remember, don't you? It had the verse inside, "The true light that lighteth every man that cometh into the world." I glanced over at her. I'm sentimental, I know, but I do love seeing her smile when she recalls something beautiful.

Mile after mile of level countryside slipped by, the expanse of sheep-dotted fields broken only by the occasional black hut where a shepherd would spend a rough night during the lambing season. Then we saw, standing on a raised knoll, a small stone church.

"Let's take a look at that," I suggested, pulling the car off the road on to the grass verge. We crossed an old brick bridge spanning the dike and followed a winding path across the field to a lych gate. Beyond the gate we found ourselves in a grassy churchyard with ancient headstones leaning at angles and in some cases nearly sunk into the ground. A few Romney Marsh sheep cropped the grass between the stones.

"Lawn mowers don't come cheaper than that! I wonder who still comes to church here. There's only the odd house for miles." I walked up to a remarkably well-kept notice board painted blue with nice gold lettering that told us, surprise, surprise, that services—either matins, evensong, or communion—were held there every Sunday.

The heavy iron-studded oak door opened without a squeak. The great hinges, stretching halfway across the door had recently been oiled. The church was clean, though musty as all old churches are, but the floor tiles were polished, and there wasn't a speck of dust to be seen anywhere.

"Somebody or some *people* really love and care for this place," said Elisabeth.

It was a tiny building, not more than forty-five or fifty feet long, oblong in shape except where the chancel narrowed. The slim, round-headed Saxon windows let in feeble light despite the splays cut in the walls around them. It was full of fascinating antiquities, but the one I liked most was a wonderful tableau of a man holding a tidbit above a begging dog. It was carved on one of the choir stall ends. "The old carvers had their bit of fun!" I said sotto voce to Elisabeth. Somehow one always speaks quietly in these venerable churches.

At the bottom end stood an old stone font with a heavy hinged lid. "They used to padlock those in medieval times so that the witches couldn't get at the "holy" water to use in their incantations," said Elisabeth.

"They'd be unlucky today," I said, raising the lid. "It's as dry as a bone!" On the table by the door was a pile of engravings of the church with a card reading, "fifty pence each, sold in aid of the repair fund. The work of Montague Billings, artist." I took one, slipped my fifty pence into the box, rolled up the art paper, and popped on a rubber band, supplied free.

There was a framed notice in beautiful classical

script on the back of the door. "Please do not leave this house of prayer where the worship of God has continued without a break for thirteen hundred years without making your petition to Him for yourself and for all those who come here. 'God is in heaven and thou upon earth: therefore let thy words be few.' Ecclesiastes 5:2." We looked at each other a little shamefaced and without a word knelt together for a few moments in the last pew. As we left, we passed a visitors' book with a biro attached by a string. I wrote in our names and address. The last entry before ours was of one "Peter John Thomson II, Denver, U.S.A."

Outside I said to Elisabeth, "Amazing! Fancy an American coming all the way from Denver to see this isolated little church."

"Perhaps he was looking for long lost ancestors," speculated Elisabeth.

"He'd have a job amongst those grave stones," I replied.

"Yes, but there may be a name in the register of baptisms." She always knows these things, being a parson's daughter.

A mile down the road we saw a sign, "Welland Manor. 13th Cent. Knight's dwelling. National Trust." It pointed down a tiny side road to the left. I stopped the car and looked at Elisabeth. "We've still lots of time. Shall we take a look?"

"Let's."

Welland Manor had no car park, so we pulled up once more on the verge by a flint and mortar wall which surrounded a lawn encircling the ancient building. In front of us was a huge American station wagon.

The manor was a small T-shaped dwelling, also built of flint and mortar and showing amazingly few signs of renovation despite its immense age. The ground floor had sunk so much that we had to go down four steps to enter the doorway to the main hall. "Hall" was a name a bit grandiose for the thirty-foot room with its small side chambers labeled "Buttery," "Kitchen," and "Store." A refectory table with forms, modern ones but fashioned in an ancient style, gave the atmosphere of the dining habits of the knight and his lady and their underlings.

At the far end we found stone steps leading crosswise to an upper floor, the "Solar," something of a luxury in those times. From there came the sound of voices, one with a local accent and the other distinctly midwest American. We went quietly aloft and found two small rooms at the end, one presumably the bedroom and the other the "garderobe." The main length of the upper story was occupied by a chapel with a raised stone dais at the far end where several narrow windows provided the sole lighting. "That would be where they placed the altar," whispered Elisabeth.

From the conversation of the two men in the chapel, we guessed that one was probably a local farmer acting as self-appointed guide, and we saw that the other was a large American tourist. He would have needed that massive station wagon to have "gotten" around in comfort. We suspected that he was probably none other than "Peter John Thomson II of Denver, Colorado." We listened spellbound as the man in rough tweeds held forth to the white-suited American. "Naow this yere room where we're a'standing', this were the bed chamber for the knoight an' 'is loidy; naow 'ere," he pointed a massive finger around the dais on which they were standing, "Oi would say was where 'e 'ad 'is dressin' chest, an' 'is bed would'a bin there." He indicated the left-hand wall.

There was a round-topped niche about a foot across in the wall at waist height. The demonstrating finger now indicated this. "Naow that was where 'e would stand 'is water jug or maybe a wine flask for their refreshment through the neight." His description hardly fitted the hollowed out "piscina" with the drainage hole in the middle where the officiating priest had washed the communion chalice, but it satisfied his American audience. Elisabeth and I looked at each other appreciatively. This was going to be far more interesting than the official leaflet we had picked up at the door. They were advancing towards us.

"Arternoon," said tweed suit.

"Good day to you, ma'am. Good day, sir," said white suit.

We smiled and murmured, "How do you do?" and retreated half into the sleeping quarters. The conducted tour was not yet complete. We waited expectantly.

"Naow this would be where the knoight and lady retired while the servants cleared away the meal at night. You see this, sir?" He led the American over to the wall where there was a stone step, a large cavity in the wall dropping in a shaft down to the ground below. The edge of a stump wall which fenced off the cavity had still an aged oak sill about two feet off the floor of the step.

"Naow this, sir, this shows that these folks what lived in former toimes 'ad lots of things which in some ways is quoite modern, only primitive, you see. Down there," he pointed over the oak sill into the depths, "the servants would loight a fire, thorns you mind, with little smoke and the risin' 'eat 'ud warm the 'ole 'ouse. Central 'eating, old English style, you might say!"

The pair moved past us down the stair, the man in tweeds parting from us with a raised finger of salute and the American nodding genially. We could see that he felt he was getting his money's worth. Their voices died away, and Elisabeth and I leaned against the wall convulsed with mirth. I suppose it was the first time an early loo had been described as a central heating system, and I had the ridiculous picture of the noble knight seated on the bar with a fire of thorns beneath.

As we too left the building, we placed a larger contribution than was our wont in the slit provided; we too had had more than our money's worth. Our tweedy friend had done his best and had demonstrated the countryman's well-known ability to improvise. The American was standing by his car, and we saw a banknote pass from him to the other and just caught his words, "Mr. Corby, I sure am grateful for your courtesy in showin' me around this interesting example of your historic past. My only regret is that my wife stayed at the inn this mornin' and did not have the benefit of your erudite exposition. I thank you." He got into his car and rumbled off down the lane. Mr. Corby lifted his chin in an acknowledgment of his generous reward and walked off down the lane in the opposite direction. We smiled happily to each other.

We went on our way again, motoring through the interminable, flat sheep country until finally we pulled up in the shingle car park near the Shambles Point Lighthouse. We were surprised to find that the sea was at least sixty yards away. We would have expected the lighthouse to have been bang on the edge of the water. In the distance we could see several fishermen with their long sea rods patiently standing by the edge of the water. We guessed there was a rapidly shelving beach and deep water near, for quite big ships were passing by very close in.

A notice on the door of the lighthouse told us that visitors would be admitted after the lunch hour.

"Okay, let's go down to the sea and have our lunch." I didn't like the idea of sending clouds of newspaper smoke over the fishermen, so we fell back on our little whistling kettle and camping Gaz stove to make our tea.

Our sandwiches went down a treat, though Elisabeth greedily ate all of hers and left none of it for me to finish. The kettle boiled, and we had a nice cup of tea. Then we leaned back against the breakwater. There came a crunching of the gravel behind us. I sat up and peered through the timbers of the breakwater. Two nattily dressed men, one older and one younger, had taken up a stance about twenty yards away and were sweeping the sea and the marsh behind us with a very professional pair of binoculars and a high-powered telescope. They had evidently not noticed us and were conversing about birds in somewhat affected tones. A very naughty thought came into my head. I ducked down again, quietly removed the whistle from the kettle, put it to my lips and blew "eet tuweet weet-weet" through it.

"Did you hear that?" asked the younger man excitedly. "Green sandpiper, only here out of breeding season."

For the second time that morning, Elisabeth and I nearly did ourselves a mischief trying not to laugh. The men moved away round the point.

"You are horrid," she accused.

"Why—*I* didn't deceive them—they deceived themselves."

When we reached the lighthouse, we found the door now open. We stopped for a moment and craned our necks backwards to see up its smooth length to the lantern bulging out on its top. The wall of the tower was ringed in black and white, and there was a balustraded rail at the top with one or two figures moving behind it round the lantern. "That must be at least a hundred feet high," I said. We went into a large ground-floor room built out as a one-story extension. There were some seats, no doubt to rest visitors wearied by the ascent to the top, and a table where one of the lighthouse staff sat at the receipt of custom. Around the walls hung old framed photographs and paintings of previous generations of keepers, going back a hundred and fifty years—tough grizzled specimens all of them, wearing uniforms, short peaked caps, and bleak countenances.

We paid our fees, and the official at the desk indicated the door to the staircase. Inside, stone steps spiraled steadily upwards. As we climbed, we were able to peep at infrequent intervals out small windows which lit the stairs. I was amazed at the thinness of the walls. "I hope this place doesn't collapse before we get down! I suppose if it's lasted a good number of years, there's a fair chance we'll make it." We must have gone up forty feet when we overtook a couple who had halted on the steps. The man was leaning against the rail and breathing heavily. He looked about my age, but he was a good three inches shorter and around three stone more in weight, I would have guessed.

He managed a brief smile. "Should 'a put a lift into this joint!" he wheezed. The woman, presumably the wife, was holding his arm and looking at him anxiously.

"Are you all right?" I asked.

"Not too dusty," he said bravely. "You can tell us what the view is like at the top when you come down. This is as far as I'm going."

I felt like saying something more, for he really did look bad, but I've learned from bitter experience not to interfere until asked. So I just nodded, and we squeezed past and went on up. "I wouldn't bet much on the state of that chap's ticker," I said when we were out of earshot.

We plowed on steadily, up and up, and finally emerged into a round chamber where there was an iron ladder leading up through an opening to the light and the observation gallery. From here the outside of the lantern windows could be cleaned. There were two other couples in the room chatting to the keeper. I gathered he was waiting for enough people to make a quorum for his dissertation on the history and functioning of the lighthouse. We evidently made up the quorum. He obviously relished his task, and he began with gusto.

"Ladies and gentlemen, I expect you may be wondering how many steps you have just climbed."

"Too blooming many," said a young fellow quietly on my left, smelling strongly of cigarette smoke.

The keeper ignored this and continued, "I will tell you in case you did not count 'em. There are 178. The light is powered nowadays by electricity from the mains, but in case of failure of the supply, we have emergency storage batteries. We have needed them at times owing to power cuts and broken power lines. We were one of the first lighthouses to use electric lighting. Would you believe it if I tell you that earlier the light, and quite a good light, came from candles! You see, even a small light when multiplied by all the mirrors is quite effective."

He continued his lecture and finally stopped for questions. A woman with the bearing of a schoolteacher asked, "Why was there a lighthouse here in the first place? Are there rocks out to sea?"

"Ah, madam, before there was ever a lighthouse, and now I'm going back many years, there had been as many as a thousand seamen lose their lives in one year off this point. You see the shambles sticks so far out into the Channel, and the water's so deep that in those far-off days mariners would run their ships into it in fog or darkness. First they had coal fires in a brazier in the top of a tower not a third as high as this one. Then they built a higher one and used the candles and mirrors. Then they had yet another taller tower and had oil lamps. Although they had built it only fifty yards from the sea, 150 years later it was nigh on 400 yards inland on account of the shingle building up on the point. So they built another. Then they decided that wasn't high enough, so they built this one. So since about 1620 there have been five lighthouses here. You can see the beach is still building up, as this was only forty yards from the edge of the water when it was built."

"How long have there been lighthouses in Britain?" The questioner was a tall cadaverous man who looked a bit like a lighthouse himself.

"Well, the Romans built the first ones. They called them 'pharos.' You can still see the remains of one at Dover." The tall man made a note in a pocket book. "Any more questions?"

There was one I wanted to ask, even though I knew it was a silly one. "As we were coming up the steps, I thought how thin the walls looked; how can they be strong enough to stand the winds?"

I think he relished having a dotty question to conclude with. "They'll stand 'em all right. Leastaways, I hope so! You see they are made of interlocking concrete rings, and they have stressing wires running through them from top to bottom which are held in tension at the base. They *are* thin, the walls, but they'll stand gales far stronger than we're ever likely to get. Now any *more* questions?" He didn't wait for some other nut to think one up, but said, "Now will you please ascend the ladder two by two, and we will see the lantern."

When our turn came, we found ourselves in a fascinating glass chamber almost filled by the great light projector. There was a marvelous view out over the Channel and the shipping which looked even nearer than on the ground, and inland we could see over a vast expanse of marsh to the distant hills standing blue in the haze. We had all the features of the light further explained to us by the keeper, had one quick trip round the balcony—which couldn't be quick enough for Elisabeth who had had her fill of heights in her youth—and having given the keeper our thanks and something more tangible, we set off down the ladder and then down the stone staircase.

We hadn't gone far when we became aware of a sound coming up which suggested the pattering of a flock of sheep combined with the chattering of a herd of monkeys. Rounding a bend, we were engulfed in a tidal wave of youth—boys and girls in the ten-to-twelve age group. Behind them came a breathless pair of adults and, in the light of one of the narrow windows, I beheld Jamie McFee and a very attractive dark-haired young lady.

Jamie was so intent on keeping tabs on the unruly mob that he did not notice us until we were almost nose to nose on the stairs. "Docco!" he gasped, halting in his bound aloft. "Fancy meeting you again!"

"No time for formalities, I imagine, but is this Katie?" She smiled, looking even prettier.

"I reckon you'd better carry on, Jamie, unless you want the keeper to have a stroke. See you for a moment at the bottom?" I asked.

"Sure, Docco, we won't be long!"

"I wouldn't be too sure!" I said, "but we'll wait for you."

We proceeded downwards, discussing the way we seemed to keep running into Jamie.

"What a nice girl he's got. I imagine that's his youth group, or whatever he calls it. I should think they have their hands full," said Elisabeth.

Emerging into the waiting room, we found a small group of people gathered around a figure sitting uncomfortably on one wooden seat with his legs on another. His head was forward, and his breath was coming in short gasps. It was the portly man from the stairs. I moved over and pushed my way through the group. Unless I was much mistaken, the poor chap was in a state of acute congestive heart failure. His wife was standing protectively over him, still holding his arm. I edged over to her and said quietly, "Would you excuse me. I am a doctor. Can I help you?"

"Oh, yes sir! Please, sir, if you would; Harold is real bad; thank God, you've come along. He's had these attacks before, but never one so bad as this. He *shouldn't* have tried those stairs, but he wouldn't listen. I didn't know what to do, and now you've come. Please help him." Her eyes filled with tears.

Elisabeth was standing quietly behind me. "Darling," I asked, "would you get my medical bag from the boot of the car?"

She was back in about three minutes, breathless. Meantime I had taken his pulse; it was rapid and thready. The assistant keeper was standing beside him now.

"Look, would you please move these people

away, and have you a screen or something to put round us?"

"Yessir." He came from a side room carrying a very old screen covered with American cloth and stood it at the back of us.

"Now come along, please. Move back; give the gentleman some air," he cried.

"Did he have any pain or tightness of the chest?" I asked the sick man's wife.

"Yes, he did, like a band round him, he said."

I managed to do a brief examination of the patient's chest, back, and blood pressure, which confirmed my first impressions. He was in congestive failure. He also had anginal pain—maybe a small coronary. He needed two things immediately—morphia to calm his whole system and relieve his pain and a diuretic to make him pass large amounts of urine to draw the fluid off his chest.

"Mrs—"

"Mrs. Dalzell, Doctor. This is Harold Dalzell."

"Mrs. Dalzell, I am Dr. Hamilton, and I practice in Wilverton on Sea; are you agreeable for me to give your husband emergency treatment—injections? I think he should be put in the hospital, but he needs something now. Okay? I have to ask you. The injections *have* a slight danger."

"Oh, yes, Doctor! Whatever you think is best."

I gave the injections and asked to use the telephone. Once more I got through to the ambulance headquarters, gave the full details of the case, made sure there would be a positive pressure oxygen apparatus on board the ambulance, and then rang the hospital in Lewes. I explained the case and who I was, and a rather tired and impatient house physician began questioning me on the condition of the patient, obviously stalling as he said they were already over full.

"Look here, I have this patient, quite a stranger to me, on the ground floor of the Shambles Lighthouse, and I consider him desperately ill. I have told you that he needs urgent admission. Are you going to accept him or not?" I was used to young overworked house physicians.

"Oh, all right, please send him in. I'm sorry, Doctor, but we already have extra beds up in the ward."

In spite of my annoyance I could feel the reluctance I had felt of old when I was a houseman and some importunate G.P. was trying to unload one of his troublesome patients on to me. I sympathized with this hard-pressed young man. Still Dalzell was in a dicey state and could collapse and die unless he got under careful supervision soon.

When I returned to the main room, I gave the thumbs-up sign to Elisabeth who was trying to comfort Mrs. Dalzell. Her husband's breathing was a little easier and his pallor less, but he was dopey now and lolled back with head dropping as he lay on the seat. I told Mrs. Dalzell what was arranged, and she smiled her thanks.

Just then the crowd of noisy youngsters erupted into the room from the stairs. They stared at us and I advanced, holding up my finger to my lips, and began shepherding them outside. Jamie and Katie appeared, bringing up the rear. I beckoned them outside as well and explained the circumstances.

"Can you hang on a few minutes? The ambulance shouldn't be all that long. We'd love a short chat."

"Sure, we'll get them organized on the shore—not enough room for crocker though, Docco! See you when you're free." They ran after their charges.

The ambulance driver descended from his seat. When he saw me, a look of sheer disbelief spread over his cheerful face.

"Not *you* again, Doctor! This is getting to be a habit!"

"Sorry, I can't help it if I'm so popular! He's in here."

I stood with Elisabeth watching the ambulance leave in a spurt of gravel.

"Hope he makes it."

"You did your best, darling."

I felt suddenly tired.

"Everything okay, Docco?" Jamie had returned, and the children were piling back into their coach, supervised by Katie. He lowered his voice, "I've only got a moment, but I did want to tell you something. You remember Benjie, the old Gypsy? Well, his premonitions were right. He lived just over a week— heart failure—but he had had me back to add a codicil to the will by which he bequeathed a good sum to your parson friend to be used for any charitable purpose of his choosing for helping Benjie to trust in the Lord at the end of his life. Nice, wasn't it? Your Mr. Ire really brought him comfort. Sorry, we'll have to get off before there's a riot, and sorry, you haven't really met Katie properly—but you will come to our wedding, won't you? Good-bye."

As the bus pulled away, we could see Katie waving to us and a lot of the kids waving too. I had quite a lump in my throat—the combined effect of Benjie, Ire, Jamie and Katie and their friendly kids and Mr. Dalzell and his wife got through to me, and somehow I didn't feel so tired now. We drove quietly on our way home through the marshes.

The Raising of the Mary Jane

It was a quiet weekend, but it was a good one. Fred gave us a rousing sermon on Sunday morning on the text, "Let us not be weary in well-doing, for in due season we shall reap, if we faint not." If, for Jesus' sake, we set out to help someone, whether it is just doing some shopping for the person or having him or her in for a cup of tea, it's no good packing up if we're not appreciated. What really counts is sticking at it, and in the end there may be a response. Perhaps the person will see that we weren't just trying to be nice. It was because we wanted to share God's love.

I thought back to Jamie McFee, who had been such a pain in the neck at our Bible class but was so very different now since he had really let Jesus into his life. I couldn't help wondering if Fred hadn't been inspired to take this line because old Benjie Boswell had at last reached out to the God whom he had neglected all his life, and there might have been someone who had done him a kindness long ago. (I was *quite* sure that the legacy Benjie had left to him wasn't what Fred meant by "reaping.") Later Fred told me that it was his son's youth work in the East End of London that was going to "reap" the benefit.

"Andy darling, I'll have to hurry back. I've just remembered I left that bread pudding cooking in the oven," Elisabeth whispered as the service ended. She slipped off. I hung on for a minute or two on the porch to be sociable. Bert introduced me to the Ferguson twins. I walked down the path with them a few steps.

"Noo, wisnae that a braw sermon?" the smaller twin Amy said breezily. "It pit me in mind o' yin I heerd the Reverend Angus McPherson gi' us lang syne in Paisley." Sister Janet said nothing but smiled agreement.

"If ye'll excuse me," said Amy, "I'll just bide a wee tae hae a wurd with the meenister."

I walked back to Seascape, and Elisabeth met me at the door. "Good job I came back. Alison's just been on the phone again. She's decided to take part of the leave that's still due her, and she wondered if she could come down again for three days. I said we'd love to have her come."

I nodded. "Didn't Fred tell us that Graham was coming down again this week too? There couldn't be any connection, could there? Not much!" Elisabeth smiled archly but didn't answer.

We were eating breakfast next morning when the usual fusillade of barking broke out as the cavalcade went by, but today we saw there was no Desmond—only Mrs. Grimshaw escorted by the wolfhounds fore and aft. I guessed his work on the nature reserve was no sinecure, and he probably arrived home too tired to make the early-morning sortie to the beach. We were right. McBeath stopped to tell us that Des was working very hard and proving quite an asset, as he already knew quite a bit about wildlife. Fred Ire told us he'd struck up quite a friendship with the lad as well.

Sure enough, Alison appeared the next morning in time for lunch in her two-seater. As we expected in the afternoon the huge figure of Graham Ire darkened the doorway. We had just finished.

"Hope I'm not upsetting your meal," he apologized. "I was wondering whether you'd like to come out for a trip in my boat tomorrow, Alison. You will excuse me for taking her away, Mrs. Hamilton, that is, if she wants to come." Alison looked at us.

"That would be a lovely idea. I'm sure you'd enjoy it, dear. Why don't you?" said Elisabeth quickly.

"Are you sure you don't mind? I've only just arrived; it seems so rude," said Alison.

When he'd gone, Elisabeth started to think aloud what food Alison ought to take.

"You mustn't worry. Graham's got a little galley built into the cabin area, and he always keeps a stock of tinned food and Nescafe and tea. All we need is some milk and bread and butter."

We evinced no surprise at this inner knowledge of the catering facilities aboard Graham's vessel. Later Alison said quite casually, "As a matter of fact I did meet Graham once in town. He took me to see the old

Boy's Club he used to work in, and we had a meal afterwards at a little Chinese restaurant he knows, and he told me all about this boat of his. It's an old lifeboat he picked up cheaply and converted himself on his holidays here. It now has small sails but also a big auxiliary motor, which he really relies on a lot. He used to take parties of boys from the club out in it. He's pretty handy at seamanship, otherwise I wouldn't go out in it! It's very seaworthy, and the boys loved it, but he's never yet persuaded his parents to go."

"I do hope you'll be all right." Elisabeth was, as usual, thinking of all the nasty things that could happen and was feeling responsible for having encouraged Alison. The girl just grinned.

"Don't worry. I'm sure Graham's a competent sailor, and he spent his last penny getting that boat seaworthy. We'll be all right, Elisabeth."

Alison had just finished her breakfast when Graham appeared. "All set? Looks a lovely day; we could make it round the headland for a mile or two and anchor and do some fishing, if you'd like to. Get you back by tea time." Alison had her kit all ready, and her eyes were bright as she said good-bye.

As they disappeared down the track, Elisabeth heaved a sigh. "I *do* hope they'll not do anything dangerous."

We did the washing up and then went into Bradham for stores as Alison's coming always made inroads into our grub. We treated ourselves to a special lunch in the delicatessen which had a few quiet tables at the far end. After that we drifted around contentedly and got back in good time for tea. Alison did not appear, so we went for a walk inland over the fields.

Dusk was falling before Alison returned, and we were both getting a bit worried by this time. Looking sunburned and tired, she apologized for being late. We could see she wasn't her normal cheerful self. We didn't ask her any questions, but just told her the water was hot if she wanted a bath. She nodded wearily and went off to the bathroom.

Elisabeth and I looked at each other. "Doesn't seem to have been a roaring success—the trip," said Elisabeth quietly. "I wonder where Graham is."

Alison had brightened up a bit when she came back into the sitting room. "Would you mind if I just popped over to the Ires' and told them not to expect Graham tonight? I'll tell you all about it over supper."

She was back in three minutes so we all sat down. After we'd had the bacon and sausages and spaghetti we'd laid on, Alison put down her fork and smiled. "Shall I tell you what happened?"

"Let's wait 'til we have had some fruit and then tell us all about it over a cup of coffee," suggested Elisabeth. "Brrr, it's getting nippy; Andy, light the fire. We might as well be cheery."

After such a beautiful day, it was getting nippy. A mist was coming up over the field, which was already half-plowed following the burning. The sticks blazed up, and the logs began to catch with that bluish light mixed with yellow flame.

"I feel better," said Alison as she stretched out her powerful but shapely legs towards the fire. "Well, I'll tell you now. We set off from the harbor and were making good headway with the wind a mere nothing in our faces. We got quite near the headland in about half an hour. I was really enjoying it. Graham let me steer. We weren't using the sails as the wind was so light we couldn't have tacked, so we just chugged along peacefully. Graham was up in the bow. Suddenly he came rushing back into the cockpit, cut the engine until it was only ticking over, and took the wheel from me.

"'Look there!' He pointed about fifty yards ahead. 'See that pole sticking out of the water?' I looked, but all I could see were several red floats bobbing about. 'I don't mean those floats; they're just lobster pot markers; no, out a bit.' I looked again and saw a sort of stick poking up from the surface of the sea. I nodded.

"'That's the top of a mast!' He sounded really excited. 'Can you see it now? There's the pulley wheel, and the halyard's still running through it—there's a boat sunk there!' He must have wonderful eyesight; we were only about eight yards away now, and I could see what he was talking about. There was the top of a mast sticking up about eighteen inches. Graham maneuvered us right up close very cleverly, dropped an anchor, and threw a rope round the mast top. Then he stopped us swinging around in the tide by dropping a heavy weight on a rope from the stern.

"'Come over here; look—you can see the shape of her hull, quite small. I should say she was about twenty feet.' I peered into the water. It's a bit muddy you know, but I could see it. He said, 'I'm going to have a go at salvaging it. Funny it's not been reported. Wonder who sank it there. Hope there's no body trapped in it.' I didn't like the sound of that, but I didn't say so.

"'Do you mind, Alison?' he asked.

"Well, to be quite honest, I was feeling a bit browned off that he'd just written off what was going to be a lovely fishing trip to try and rescue some rotten old boat, but I just said it was okay.

"'I'll have to go back to the harbor for some gear, but I'll tie a buoy onto the mast top, and that means we've claimed the right to try and salvage it.' He hauled out quite a big metal ball he kept in the forepeak and lashed it to the mast top. Then we went like the clappers back to the harbor, and he explained what he was going to do. It sounded a bit risky, but he seemed to know what he was doing. We moored up, and he rushed into the shed there and came back with a lot of nylon rope and his scuba diving gear. On the way to the wreck he told me that there was no time to lose—the tide had turned an hour or two back, and he must get hitched up to the wreck before it went down too far. Then we'd have to stay there 'til the tide was well in again before we could get it off the bottom. I didn't really understand what he was talking about, but I hoped for the best."

"Have some more coffee," offered Elisabeth.

"Thanks. Well, I was steering again, and Graham was down below getting the diving gear ready, and I could see there was someone in a rowboat out there looking at Graham's buoy, so I called him up to have a look. 'Oh, that's all right,' he told me. 'That's only old Loader after his lobster pots. Expect he's wondering what's going on.' As we came up we hailed him, and

Graham told him what he was going to do. Funny, it was as if he didn't like it. I suppose he was a bit fed-up that someone was mucking around his lobster-catching area. He is an odd bloke, isn't he—sort of miserable-looking. Graham told him his idea was to lift the sunken boat under his big lifeboat and tow it under water past the harbor and beach it on the sandy shore beyond. The lobster man listened and then started his engine and began heading back to the beach.

"Though I was still feeling a bit fed-up myself, I had to admire Graham. We anchored as before and tied up to the mast. He got on his gear and dived with a length of rope tied on to a cleat on the deck of our boat, and I could see him feeling around below, about ten feet down now. He brought up the loose end of the rope as he surfaced on the other side of our boat, pulled it tight, and tied it to a shackle. Then he repeated the whole process farther astern, clambered back on board, took off his gear, dried himself, got dressed in the cabin, and calmly said we'd have lunch. While we were eating in the cockpit, and it was lovely out there in the sunshine, every quarter of an hour or so he got up and tightened all the four rope ends. I washed up, and he dried, and then we just waited. We waited and waited, but I didn't really mind. The sunken boat was now slung beneath us. The idea was that when the tide started to come in again, it would lift us and, with any luck, the sunken boat would have to come off the bottom with us as we rose.

"It worked! We began to feel a funny swaying movement. Of course we'd had to lengthen the anchor cables too as the tide rose, but this was different. Then we could actually see the boat swinging about almost beneath us. 'Time to go!' said Graham. He started the engine—and we were underway! We had to take it carefully with this dead weight dragging us around below, but we made fair time back and then—disaster struck!" Alison was quite enjoying this and made a dramatic stop.

"Go on—what happened?" Elisabeth had got quite excited, a most unusual phenomenon.

"We-ell, we got grounded in the Bradham Channel out to sea! Graham was really worried about blocking the harbormaster's seaway. By sheer strength he managed to tighten the ropes a tiny bit, and then we put the engine full ahead and—she came off. It was now fully high tide, and Graham drove us in towards the beach as far as he dared. The boat was grating on the bottom. We loosed it off, anchored, and Graham tied the weight to one of the rope ends still attached to the boat below, and chucked it in. Then he tied his buoy to another.

"'Have to hope she stays put in the sand,' he said. Then he told me he'd run me back to the harbor and row back himself across the Bradey in his rubber dinghy with a sleeping bag. He wanted to stay near the boat. He knows the farmer whose land comes down near the beach and was going to borrow a tractor to haul the boat out of reach of the next tide. He asked me if I would mind going back by myself and telling his parents what he's doing. Then he apologized for spoiling our day. So there we are." Alison put her cup down. "I'll just wash these up, and then you won't mind if I go to bed? I feel a bit tired."

"You'll go straight off now," I said.

Alison stifled a yawn. "Thanks so much. Goo'-night. Hope I haven't bored you."

"Don't be silly, dear. What a story!" Elisabeth took her cup and gave her a kiss. "Sorry it didn't turn out quite the way you expected." I wondered what Elisabeth had expected.

Next morning we could hear Alison moving around when I was getting the tea. Elisabeth took her in a cup. I could hear them talking through the wall. "Elisabeth, could I ask a favor? Would you mind if I took my car and went round by the road bridge and took Graham some grub and a thermos of coffee? The poor lad won't have had anything since last night." Elisabeth said of course she could. We had a very quick prayer and reading that morning and had breakfast laid on in double-quick time. We packed Alison up some bacon sandwiches and fixed the thermos, and she took off in her car. We arranged to follow her up a bit later.

About ten we came down the farm track, parked the car, and walked down to the beach. The two of them were working away on quite a nice-looking little cabin cruiser lying heeled over at an angle in the sand. It was scraped and muddy. Graham spotted us first.

"Come and look at the *Mary Jane*, and wait 'til I tell you something!"

He had awakened in the early hours and heard someone moving about on the boat. He sat up and shouted and could just see a figure jump off the boat and run like mad up the beach. He'd tried to pursue, but got his feet tangled in the sleeping bag and fell over. By the time he was up, the figure had disappeared, but he heard a car start and drive away up the track past the farm. That was only the beginning. As soon as it was light, he had begun a careful examination of the boat. He first scraped off the mud and found the name *Mary Jane,* and then he saw that there was a large hole in the timbers near the keel and guessed that she had run onto a sunken rock out near the cliff.

It looked as if the man or men on board had only managed to get off in a rubber dinghy without collecting any gear because he found a locker in the cabin which had a bundle of French bank notes in it, all sodden with seawater. He wanted to see how much damage there was to the hull from the inside, and he'd pulled up some of the floor boards over the gash and found—a large plastic bag and in it a whole heap of little plastic bags containing a white powder!

"Do you know what I think?" he asked excitedly. "I think it's drugs—probably heroin."

"Hasn't there been some talk of heroin-smuggling somewhere along the Sussex coast? D'you think this could be it?"

"The first thing you've got to do is get to a police station and let them get the county drug squad to examine it," I said.

"I'll take you in my bus," offered Alison.

They left carrying the plastic bag and a bundle of sodden papers from the locker and the notes. We reckoned that whoever had been giving the boat the once-over in the night wouldn't find much now, but we said we'd come over again and see that no one interfered with it. We went to the Ires', told them the state of play, and did this and that to fill the time between nipping over to keep a wary eye on the boat. Nobody seemed to go near it. We couldn't really settle to anything, and late in the afternoon Graham and Alison showed up.

"Whew! What a day!" Graham sat down on the drop-end settee beside Alison. I thought anxiously about its aged springs.

"It was heroin all right. Put the cat among the pigeons, that did. Had the drug squad buzzing like flies!" We gathered from his mixed metaphors that things were on the move. "I think some men will be down going over the boat already," he said excitedly.

"You must be ready for a good supper I should think; if I fix it with your parents, d'you think they'd mind if you had it here? There might be some clues we could talk over."

Graham nodded. "It's very kind of you."

"I'll go and ask them and perhaps go on and try and pick up a couple of lobsters from old Loader if he hasn't shut up shop. Would you like that? We're partial to them. Never get them somehow at home."

"That would be lovely, if you don't mind," said Alison.

It was okay with the Ires. They were used to their son's erratic ways. I left it to Graham to tell them his news. We had to make do with scrambled eggs for supper though. I found the potter's shut and could get no response to some loud knocking at the door.

"Ye'll not get no reply there, sir," declared the old fisherman in the next cottage who was standing smoking a pipe in his doorway. "I seed 'im go off in 'is van 'bout four."

I thanked him and walked back home.

As we were finishing supper, we turned on the radio for the weather and the seven o'clock news summary. There was a travel warning. There had been a serious accident south of Tonbridge. "A small motor van entered the highway almost in the path of a heavy goods vehicle and was hit from behind, killing the driver of the van. The driver of the truck was unhurt but was suffering from shock. The police have not given the name of the dead man until the relatives have been informed. There is only single-lane traffic at present and a tail back for a mile. It is hoped the road will be cleared within the hour."

"I'm so glad you weren't going back to town this evening, Alison," said Elisabeth.

I kept quiet. I had a queer feeling about that van and the driver. Next morning both Alison and Graham left for "the smoke." It was the day after that that the news broke. The radio and the papers were full of it. My sense of foreboding was justified. The man in the van was Loader. His van had been full of crates of pottery figures, apparently inadequately packed. Many were smashed, and in their fragments police found packets of heroin. What was more, they found invoices for pots and figures from a shop in Carnaby Street. The story about Loader's name being withheld for the sake of the relatives was somewhat devious. The police simply did not want to give anyone warning. They raided the Carnaby Street shop, found a quantity of heroin and other drugs, and discovered a Frenchman and an Englishman hiding in an upstairs room. Among the dried-out papers from the *Mary Jane* was the certificate of ownership in the name of the Englishman.

The *piece de resistance* was the evidence that Loader had hidden the drugs for transport from Bradham Harbor to Carnaby Street in pottery lobsters! The carapace of the back of the lobster had been fired separately from the underparts and glued to the lower parts out of sight with a firm adhesive. To recover the packets of heroin, however, the Carnaby Street shop owner would have had to break the figurines. The heroin-containing lobsters would have had an identifying mark on their stick-on labels.

The day we got the news a police car was standing outside Loader's shop for some hours. They found one mislaid packet of heroin behind various articles at the back of a cupboard. The owners of the Carnaby Street shop, Eric Crabnell and Henri Laporte, were charged at Bow Street Magistrates' court. Loader had gone to a higher court.

We were getting towards the end of our holiday, but all we felt fit for after the excitement was a quiet day on the beach. Elisabeth and I were walking down the long stretch of sand when she said, "Don't you feel sad, darling, that we never were able to get near to poor Loader? What a way to go to meet God. He had had such a sad life. He must have just sunk into bitterness and wrong."

"Yes, love, but we only saw him for moments in

the shop, and all we were thinking of was buying lob-sters. Lobsters! That's it! Nobody's come up with an explanation for how Loader got the heroin from the blokes in the *Mary Jane*. He's never been seen going out at night in his boat, so that's it!" I said again.

"What do you mean? He couldn't have taken out the pottery lobsters with him!"

"No! But what about lobster *pots?* The blokes in the *Mary Jane* come in the dark, haul up a lobster pot or two, insert the big plastic bags and obstruct the opening so lobsters can't get in. Loader's warned of the drop, goes out next morning, picks up his lobsters *and* the packets as well, and stows them in a bag. I'll phone the police station when we get back. I know it's only a theory, but it may help them to make the pros-ecution case stick if they can demonstrate in court how the chain could have been completed!"

When I phoned, the police sergeant seemed a bit slow in the uptake, but he took down the points and said he would pass them on. We spent the last day or two cleaning up Seascape. Even I began to look for-ward to getting back into harness, and Elisabeth in her heart of hearts was never a hundred percent at peace away from home, telephone or no telephone. On the day of departure I took the keys round to Bert, said good-bye, and we drove off down the track for the last time that summer.

On the Receiving End

I couldn't make it out. I drove along with Elisabeth dozing by my side. I was a bit weary too, but that wasn't what was bothering me. I don't suffer from car-sickness, but I was beginning to feel queasy. I didn't want to worry Elisabeth. She needed the rest. We made it home without my throwing up, but by the time I had heaved the luggage out of the boot and into the house, I was feeling really rotten.

"Let's have a break and a cup of tea," suggested Elisabeth. "I'll pop the kettle on." In a few minutes she came back into the lounge with the tray. She looked at me and frowned.

"You all right, darling? You look pretty awful; what's the matter?"

"Not so good. Sorry, I don't think I can take any tea; do you mind if I just pop into bed for a bit?"

"Darling, are you *really* feeling ill?" She was now looking so concerned that I tried to take a grip on myself.

"See how I feel after a lie down." I walked slowly out; the pain in my tum was definitely worse, and I was feeling feverish. Elisabeth helped me to lie down and covered me with a rug. I dozed off for only about fifteen minutes. Then I sat up with difficulty, got a thermometer out of the bedside table drawer, and, bugs or no bugs, stuck it straight into my mouth. When I took it out, I saw my temperature was 101.4°. The pain too seemed to be localizing now. I pressed myself. Ouch! It was definitely low down in the right iliac fossa, and my tum was harder there than anywhere else.

"Elisabeth," I called. She came in, drying her hands. "Love, I'm pretty certain I've got appendicitis."

"Oh, Andy dear, have you really? What do you think we ought to do?"

"I'm afraid you'll have to ring up the surgery and get one of them to come out and see me. *They'll* be pleased—expecting me back on Monday and now mucking up *their* holidays." Elisabeth looked quietly at me and went out to the phone. I could only hear snatches of what she said when she got through to the surgery, but it seemed to take quite a time. She came back.

"Darling, Mrs. Banbury was so nice. She was very concerned to hear you weren't feeling well, and she'll get you seen as soon as she possibly can. The trouble is, it's Graham's weekend off, and he's taken his kiddy to the Dolphinarium at Brighton. Donald's in the surgery, but she said if you weren't too bad, could you hang on 'til the surgery's finished? It shouldn't be long. He has only two patients to see, and then she'd send him straight round. I said I thought it would be all right." She looked at me questioningly, her eyes full of concern. She came over and softly pushed my hair off my face. "*Was* that all right? I'll ring again if you want me to."

I shook my head and said nobly in a long-suffering voice, "It's okay. I can stick it," and made a wry face. In fact I was feeling quite a bit worse.

Twenty minutes later Donald walked in with Elisabeth at his heels. Donald is a dour Scot with a quirky sense of humor.

"Hello, Andy. Not had enough holiday? What's all this about an appendix?"

I gave a weak grin, which terminated rapidly as it seemed to bring on a worse spasm in my guts. Donald didn't miss it. He sat down on the edge of the bed while I said my piece. He pursed his lips, pulled down the bedclothes, and very gently laid a hand on my abdomen. When he got down on the right, I couldn't help wincing. He frowned.

He examined me rectally and took my pulse and my temperature. "Hhmm," he said as he read the thermometer, "101.8°, pulse 110. You've got an appendix, or I'm a Dutchman. I'll ring the hospital." He went out, followed by Elisabeth, who was now looking really worried. I waited. He seemed to be taking a time too. At last he returned.

"Sorry, Andy, they haven't got a single surgical bed left at the sanatorium, but they'll admit you to

Brendan Hospital, and old MacFarlane is operating there now, so he'll see you more or less at once. Sorry," he said again.

"Don't worry. I'll be fine there. It's a nice little place. I was in there once before years ago for a tonsillectomy. Nearly closed the hospital—I developed scarlet fever!" I smiled weakly.

Donald's face signified, "You're a right one!"

The ambulance took half an hour. As they were shutting the doors, I waved to Elisabeth and tried to smile. She had tears in her eyes as she waved back. It was a swift trip, and soon I was being installed in a small room in the ward. Then in came Sister Marjorie, still in charge of the ward, but now she had gone gray and her face had become lined.

"Well, Doctor, here we are again! Now you're not going to close down my ward a second time, I hope."

"I'll try not to, Sister, but I warn you, I've had a bit of ticker trouble in the interim, so I hope I don't pass out on you. You'll have to be very kind to me." She looked out of the corner of her eye at me while she did the temperature and pulse-taking all over again and recorded them on my chart hanging on the end of the bed.

"Dr. MacFarlane will see you in a minute or two. We've just had his last case back from the theater." I composed myself to wait for the inevitable reexamination. In came MacFarlane, a tall cadaverous man with wispy, graying hair, followed by his house surgeon, both in white theater trousers and singlets, white coats over the top. I liked MacFarlane. He had some way-out views, but he was a rattling good operator.

"Hello, Hamilton isn't it? Let's have a look at you." When he finished, he shrugged his shoulders. "Appendix, all right. Have it out straight away; when did you last have food?"

"Not since about seven o'clock—only a cup of tea and a slice of toast."

"Right. Handwell, give him his premed and get him prepped." He went out.

The last thing I remember was simply putting myself in God's hands, aware that anesthetics and operations were not the best thing for someone whose ticker was a bit dodgy. Then free of pain, I drifted off into oblivion . . .

I stared at the space beside me. The next-door patient was gone and his bed with him. The opposite side of the ward where there had been an old man was empty too. *Odd*, I thought. *They'll be taking me down to theater soon.* I moved in the bed, and a nasty dragging pain caught me in the right side. I put my hand under the bedclothes and encountered—Elastoplast! "By gum! They've done it!" I breathed a heart-felt, "Thank you, Lord."

I dropped off to sleep again. When I opened my eyes, there sitting side by side, grinning widely, were our two sons, Peter and Barney. Peter had come 350 miles just to be with his dad. I put it down to the painkiller, as I'm not given to crying, but the tears ran down my cheeks and off my chin before I could stop them.

"Want to see your appendix?" Barney asked tactfully. He crossed the ward and brought me a jar with a repulsive worm-like structure floating in Formalin.

"See that?" He pointed to a black area on the tail of the specimen. "Gangrenous—they just got that out in time."

"It's nice and quiet here in intensive care," said Peter.

So *that* was it! No wonder there weren't any other patients around. I wondered if my ticker had caused them any worry during the operation. For the first time I became aware of the cardiac monitor screen standing to the left of my bed head and of the wires stuck by sticky pads to my chest. The lads couldn't stay long, as they'd both got journeys ahead of them, and they'd still had to give Elisabeth a look-in.

The staff were very patient with me while I was under their care. For two days I lived in a passive state of euphoria, punctuated by injections, blanket baths, sips of water, and passage to and fro of urine bottles and the longer intervals between dear Elisabeth's visits which she could only make when she got a lift. All the time the saline dripped quietly from the hanging plastic bag into my vein. But it was too good to last.

"Moving you back to the main ward today," said Sister Marjorie. "Your ticker has been behaving in exemplary fashion. You can have a bit of lunch first too, toast and tea. We're taking down the drip."

"Call that lunch, Sister? I'm starving! I could eat a horse."

"Well, you're not going to. Toast and tea it is. You ought to know the drill."

I grinned and thought of those tiny little stitches in my caecum that were all that stood between me and a perforated gut. After my "lunch," I was whisked off down the corridor which was biting cold, being roofed above but open at the sides. I'd been determined, true to principle and my Scottish instincts, not to have private treatment. Also I determined I was going to be one of the crowd, forget I was a doctor, and just see what it was like to be on the receiving end. But my heart sank a bit as I was plonked down slap in the middle of a busy ward with a poor, confused aged man on my right, groaning continually and calling for the nurse, and on my left a chap who simply sat on his bedside chair, permanently silent, contemplating his slippers.

To my relief I learned that I was going to be moved straightaway to the top end of the ward, which was partly separated from the general ward by a half partition. I was assessed now to be a straightforward convalescent case. The only snag was that the telly was at that end, which caused it to become congested at peak-viewing times. I was one of six in that privileged area. I felt like an interloper.

As he went out to the bathroom, the chap from the next bed announced to the others, "We've got a stranger in the camp, mates."

I was a mite put out. When he returned, I asked, "Meaning me?"

"Don't worry, mate, we're all strangers here." He grinned pacifically. I realized he was only trying to be funny, so I grinned in return. He was Fred, who had had part of his insides removed. Next to him was Bert, a real Hoxton cockney and a former regimental feather-weight boxing champion—a hernia case. Opposite them was Daniel, a brave, elderly man who had such chronic emphysema that he had to have bronchodilators in oxygen night and morning to help him get his breath. Next to him was Kim, a cheery lad of sixteen who walked gaily round the ward with a plastic hangbag carrying urine which came from a tube in his bladder, just like half a dozen elderly men on the ward. Last there was Bob, a burly fellow whose ailment remained a mystery to me throughout. He turned out to be a proper barracks-room lawyer who knew the answer to everything and told me a lot of things about Africa which were very interesting—and entirely wrong. I managed to keep it dark for some time what my calling was, but they found out in the end, and from thereon treated me with a mixture of friendly awe and mild suspicion as "one of *them*."

Despite the fact that my internals seemed permanently and painfully sealed, I laughed so much on that ward that I could easily have burst my stitches. Kim really got it from Bert and Fred after visiting hour one evening. As the doors opened, there was a sudden pattering of feet and six charming young ladies dashed in and sat all round his bed in an admiring ring. He didn't know which one to talk to first, and his explanation afterwards that they were just from his youth club brought only scorn.

"Right flirt you are—six girls at once, oh dear!" said Bert.

Next day Bob was discharged. His bed was taken by a day case. Bert and Fred turned their attentions to him and let poor Kim off the hook.

"Wot you 'avin' done, mate?" Bert asked him.

"Just a skin job," said the newcomer.

"Oh, a snip." Fred nodded. "Now *you* want to watch it, mate. You never know what you can lose once old Brindley starts 'is snippin'.'"

"Yes, an' them scissors of 'is ain't none too sharp neither," cut in Bert.

"You should 'ave seen the last bloke 'ere wot 'ad a snip—all bandages 'e wos—couldn't 'ardly see 'is face when 'e come back to the ward!"

The victim took it all in good part and went down to theater patently cheered up, which was really the objective of the humorists all the time.

From time to time as I lay in bed, I wondered seriously how real my discipleship had been among these genuine workaday folk. Gradually I realized that what really mattered was not doing a lot of talking but just *being*—being unselfish, doing small helpful things for patients, being genuinely grateful for all the unstinting service the nurses gave us all the time. Maybe they weren't all oil paintings, but their real beauty was in their care for us. The nights were long, but I found a wonderful comfort in repeating familiar hymns to myself. My favorite was "How sweet the name of Jesus sounds in a believer's ear; it soothes his sorrows, heals his wounds, and drives away his fear."

Kim was discharged at last, and a retired ambulance driver, a methodical ward-pacer, was given his bed. We quickly became buddies and talked long and earnestly about matters common to ambulance men and doctors, and many other subjects. He beat me regularly at chess too.

"Yes," he said one day as we were drinking our midmorning tea at the table, "I reckon the world situation's almost as bad as in the war. I don't see any future for mankind with nuclear warfare possible at any time."

"I'd feel the same if I didn't have faith in God," I said quietly.

"God! How can you believe in Him with all the horrors that go on in the world? I used to believe in Him, went to church, and Boys' Brigade and all that, but I was in Eastbourne when a doodle-bug hit the children's hospital. That finished it for me."

There wasn't an easy answer, so I didn't try to find one. I sat silently for some minutes. Then I said, "Suffering *is* a tremendous problem; I can't explain it, but when you see God suffering as His son dies on a cross, you know He has the answer, and we can trust Him."

"The chuck wagon's through the pass," announced Bert, spotting the electric car towing several covered food containers into the ward. There the conversation had to rest.

Monday came round at last, and MacFarlane examined me again. "Home for you tomorrow," he said. I thanked him sincerely for his care and began thinking of what I could send him as a token of my gratefulness.

Long before two, my discharge time, all my bits and pieces were in a plastic bag, and I sat on the edge of my bed waiting for my daughter and—freedom! Her tall, lissom figure came striding down the ward. At thirty she looked twenty. I felt proud of her.

"Hello, Dad, all set? Here's your gear." I shoved it slowly on, conscious that the ward was taking more notice of Sarah than me. I shook hands all round, Sarah grabbed my plastic bag, we went down the ward, and I went into the nurses' room with many thanks and a big box of chocolates. Soon we were spinning down the country lanes home to Elisabeth.

I went early to bed and there, lying by Elisabeth, thankful, content, bathed and full of lovely home food (an improvement on what had been brought by "chuck wagon through the pass"), I said a prayer of grateful thanks.

Next morning Donald came round after surgery. He was genuinely uncompromising. "Now get this straight," he said fairly. "You're having at least two more weeks off and then, and only then, if you feel up to it, you can do some surgeries to start with. Okay?"

"But, Donald, I really don't feel too bad—"

He held up his hand. I could see he was enjoying bossing me about. "Nothing doing—don't want you collapsing a second time. See you."

He went out the door, and I heard him talking to Elisabeth in the hall. We agreed, Elisabeth and I, that after all it was good sense, and I made the most of the time by getting mobile again and walking in the fresh air.

Last Appointment

My two weeks had gone by. The holiday and even my appendicitis were now like snapshots in an album, already in the back of the mind, only to be revived at odd times if we happened to open the album again. It was my first morning for the surgery, and I was once more busily engaged with my porridge when the post came. Elisabeth kindly got up to collect it. There were two letters addressed to "Dr. and Mrs. Hamilton" and one to "Mrs. A. Hamilton." She took that one and generously gave the other two to me. She got hers open first.

"Oh hurray! Listen to this; it's from Jenny. 'I hope you will be pleased to hear that Alison is engaged to Graham Ire whom she met and had some adventures with while she was down staying with you and Andrew at Bradham Harbor. He seems such a nice young man, but, goodness—what a size! I'm afraid they won't be able to get married before he leaves his theological college and gets a curacy.'

"Isn't it lovely; I was so afraid she was put off by that episode over the *Mary Jane*. Who are your letters from?"

"I was going to tell you, but you got in first. This one," I waved a printed card, "is from a Mr. and Mrs. Bernard Waterman. It's an invitation to the wedding of their daughter Katie to Mr. James McFee in Lewes in November. I liked her, didn't you? We must think about a wedding present for them. I wonder if Jamie's dad will get there. He's in a wheelchair. You know, he runs that telephone answering service for doctors here. Did I ever tell you how I rang him up once and a voice said, 'Shut up! Go away!' and then McFee came on the line and apologized for his Myna bird?"

"Yes, darling, you *have* told me, *several* times, but who was that second letter from?"

"I haven't opened it yet." I slit open the letter with my table knife and looked at the name at the end. "It's from Bert Pettigrew. He says, 'I thought you'd like to know that the Johnsons, your missionary friends with their toddler, really enjoyed their week at Seascape. Jean went in after they'd gone and found everything spick and span. We've turned off your fridge, in fact all the electricity, at the meter. So don't forget to tell any-one else you have coming in. What a turnout that was over the drug running! It was very sad that Loader was so involved. There was always something odd about him. Things haven't settled down yet; it's the first thing folk talk about when we meet in the village.

Did you see those crooks got ten years each at the Old Bailey?

"'The Ires have started a home Bible study. We meet there every fortnight, mostly folk you know along the Ridge here. Quite a bunch. There are the twins and the Billinghursts and guess who! Young Desmond! He seemed to drink it all in and asked some really intelligent questions. We are doing the adventures of St. Paul in the Acts, and old Fred fairly brings it to life. We talked about St. Paul's conversion on the Damascus road last week. Desmond doesn't seem to mind the rest of us being a lot of old fogies. He walked a little way back with Jean and me, and he told me that he'd come because of something you'd said when you were birdwatching together once.

"'We are looking forward to seeing you in the not too distant future.'"

"How kind of him to send us all the news, especially about Desmond. I'm so glad, but I'm afraid he will break off attending the Bible study when he goes for his Nature Reserve Warden's course; I wonder if we could put him in touch with a live youth group where he's going."

I swigged down the last of my coffee quickly, got up, kissed Elisabeth, and went straight out to the car. I was going to be late for surgery if I didn't hurry. I was still being let down lightly into visiting by the partners. As I drove along, I sang loudly, "All people that on earth do dwell, sing to the Lord with cheerful voice. . . ." I couldn't help letting it rip. There had been so many things in those letters to make me sing.

On my desk were the usual pile of patients'

record cards and some special letters. Among them was a hospital report some days old. It was about Mrs. Elwood. She had been admitted very quickly as an urgent case with the diagnosis of cancer of the rectum. Sadly, at operation the growth could not be removed, and there was secondary spread. All they could do was to give her a short circuit by a colostomy. Complications had followed, and two weeks later, without being discharged from hospital, she had died peacefully.

I felt that it was in the kindness of God that she and her family had been spared the pain of a long, drawn-out deterioration before the inevitable end. I made a note to write a letter to the family as I always did, but it was with heavy heart that I pressed the bell for the first patient.

Two hours later I called in the last patient, and in came old Jos Blagdon. He gave me one of his one-sided Gypsy grins.

"Ullo, Doctor. Glad ter see yer back."

"Hullo, Jos; sit down and tell me all about yourself."

When I had given him his routine checkup and found him going along nicely, I wrote the last note and leaned back in my chair. "Well, I got along to your fair, but I'm afraid I was too late to see the greis; that was all finished, but I had a fair old adventure on the roundabout!"

"I knows all about that, Doctor. 'Eard it all on the gripevine. But did you know old Benjie Boswell died soon after? Sad that; good old mate o' mine 'e wuz; 'eard tell 'e got religion too at the end."

A Taste of His Own Medicine

"Yes, Jos, I knew. He put his trust in Jesus, and he died in peace, I'm sure."

Jos didn't say anything for a moment. He seemed deeply moved. Then he rose to go and stuck out his hand.

"Anyways, Doctor, you 'ad a nice change and rest, I 'opes."

"You could say that—apart from attending three emergencies, going out in the lifeboat to a Spanish sailor, and ending up in hospital myself with an appendicitis."

He looked at me. "Proper busman's 'oliday, eh, Doctor?"

158